RE-WRITING CHRISTMAS

KYRA LENNON

To Kallia,

Thank you for being a huge support and a champion for readers of all ages!

Lots of love

Kyra Lennon
xxx

Book Cover by Clare Bentley

ACKNOWLEDGMENTS

As always, a team of people came together to make this book happen! Clare Bentley, Katie Smith, Clare Dugmore, Emma Davis, and Sophie Mitchell are absolute heroes for beta reading for me, and extra love to Clare B for the beautiful book cover!

Huge thanks also to Irish Ink Publishing for the lovely formatting! I appreciate your help and speedy turnaround times!

To Richard, my long-suffering other half – thank you for putting up with my crazy late nights through November while I worked on this book almost non-stop. I love you!

Next up, to the badass members of the Write Here, Write Now Community – sprinting with you guys is why this book exists, and I adore every single one of you.

Finally, to those of you who have bought this book – I can't express how much it means that you want to read my words. You have my endless love and gratitude. <3

CHAPTER 1

NOVA

My front door closed behind me with a click, and I leaned against it, relishing the warmth of my home after coming in from the biting air outside.

Thank God for central heating.

I was already counting down the days until the end of term, when I wouldn't have to go out in the frigid winter mornings and could instead stay snuggled up in bed. In just over a week, there would be no more teaching for fourteen whole days. No more early starts and long days, only the promise of everything the most magical time of year could bring.

I didn't take off my coat and scarf because I was going straight back out to see my neighbour; I'd only come into the house to drop off my bag. On Friday afternoons, once I was home from work, we had a long-standing arrangement that I would go to hers for tea and biscuits; a sort of end-of-the-week treat. This particular day, she'd promised warm mince pies with clotted cream—a true Devonshire favourite.

June had been so kind to me when I'd moved in next door eighteen months ago, and she had recently lost her husband, Trevor. He'd had a heart attack six months ago, and this was going to be her first Christmas without him. She was extremely fit for a woman in her mid-seventies, but in the early stages of her grief, she hadn't wanted to do even the most basic of things, so I'd stepped in to get her shopping and cooked for her when she was struggling. Although things had improved, the festive season had brought her grief to the surface again, and I checked in on her regularly.

Jingling my keys, I opened the front door and locked it on my way out, popping the key into my coat pocket. I wrapped my coat tighter around me as I rushed down my garden path and then hurried up June's, eager to get somewhere warm again and more than ready for the treats awaiting me.

I reached up to knock on the door just as it opened, and I was met by a man I'd never seen before. I stumbled back, almost falling off her front step.

The tall, dark-haired man frowned as he took me in while I caught my balance. He didn't even try to steady me. He was clearly not expecting me any more than I was expecting him.

"Can I help you?" he asked.

Words failed me for a moment as I looked at him. He was extremely tall and stocky, and his eyes were a piercing blue. A scruffy beard adorned his chin, and he wore black jeans and a blue denim jacket over a white t-shirt. If it weren't for the frown causing a deep furrow in his brows, he would have been gorgeous. But he was also surly and abrupt, so I pushed that thought away immediately.

"I… Is June here?" I asked as his eyes surveyed me with distrust. What the hell was his problem?

"Who are you?"

Who are you? I wondered, taken aback by his rude tone. He was looking at me like I was some annoying salesperson, but I was pretty sure I didn't have that appearance. I was barely wearing any makeup, and although I was still dressed in my child-friendly work outfit of a knee-length black skirt and a blue jumper under my long black coat, my hair was falling out of its updo. I was sure I looked too dishevelled to appear saleswoman-like.

"Donovan, get out of the way."

Some of my irritation eased as I heard June's voice, and she appeared at the man's side. Her small frame tried to oust him from the doorway, and he shuffled over to accommodate her.

June was a tiny woman with a big personality; her smile lit up her face when she saw me. "Come on in, dear. Don't mind him."

The man—Donovan, apparently—looked down at her. "Nan, you haven't seen me in ten years and you already want me out of here?" His voice held a hint of teasing, but his eyes told a different story. A distant look suggested he didn't want to be there anyway.

She rolled her eyes behind her rectangular-framed glasses. "Move. You're letting all the warm air out of the house. Besides, you were just going out anyway."

I didn't consider that the car I'd parked behind on the road outside might belong to someone visiting June. Unfamiliar cars parked outside often, grabbing any space they could find. It was rare for anyone to visit June, though, aside from the few friends she had who lived a couple of streets away, but most of them didn't drive.

Wait. Did he say 'nan'? I searched my brain, trying to recall if she had ever mentioned Donovan before.

"I'm going to run into town and pick up the clotted cream you forgot," he said, stepping down onto the same step as me and looking me over once again. "I won't be long."

He left before any introduction could be made, prompting June to open the door wider so I could come in.

The warm air enveloped me immediately, and I let out a sigh of relief, rubbing my hands together. Smiling again, June said, "Get your coat off and I'll make some tea."

Once we were settled in her cosy living room with our drinks, I said, "So… that was your grandson?"

June nodded at me from her comfy armchair. "Yes. That's Donovan." I couldn't quite gauge her tone or expression, but I wasn't sure whether I should pry.

"I'm sorry. If I'd known you were having a visitor…"

She waved her hand dismissively. "*I* didn't know I was having a visitor, but even so, nothing would stop our Friday afternoon chats." Her warm smile relaxed me, but I still couldn't help wondering why he'd looked at me so suspiciously. Maybe, where he was from, people didn't just pop in to see their neighbours. "Honestly, I was so surprised to see him that I didn't get a second to tell him you were coming over for mince pies. He won't mind, though. It's been a long time since he was in Dawlish, and he was eager to get a taste of Gay's Creamery clotted cream again."

From the way he'd looked at me, it seemed as if he minded a lot, but I didn't say so. Couldn't argue with his logic on food, though. If there was one thing I'd missed when my parents moved us to Exeter when I was a kid, it was the taste of the local cream. Luckily, we were close enough to drive down to get some now and again.

"So, did he grow up here?" I asked.

He looked around my age, probably a little older, but it was a small town, and I would have remembered if we had ever been in the same school, especially with a name as distinctive as Donovan.

"No, not really," June said. "He was born here, but his parents moved to Cornwall when he was three, and then they moved to Italy when he was twelve. Donovan has been travelling the world since he was eighteen. This is the first time he's set foot in England since then."

"So, you haven't seen him in...?"

"Ten years. He barely kept in touch, but I can't hold that against him." She sighed. "He didn't really grow up having me and his grandad around because Trevor and I lived in Manchester when he was born. We moved here when he was eleven, so he didn't get much regular time with us before they left the country. I never expected him to worry about his old gran and grandad when he was having adventures."

I wasn't sure I agreed. I'd loved my grandparents and visited them once a week, sometimes more when I could. I was unlucky to have lost them all at a young age, and I would have done anything to have them back.

"So, is he moving here or just passing through?" I asked.

"Just passing through." A wistful look crossed her eyes. "I think his parents guilted him into spending Christmas with me since they're away on a cruise. They booked it before..." She paused, swallowing hard as tears brimmed in her eyes. "Before Trevor died. They didn't want me to be alone."

I reached over to squeeze her hand. June and Trevor had been the most adorable older couple. Most couples quit holding hands when they're in public once the honeymoon period is over, but not them. Their hands were always joined, even for a quick shopping trip in town. Love and adoration absolutely oozed from them, and June's grief was almost palpable sometimes. She handled it well mostly, but the loneliness got to her more often than she let on.

"You wouldn't have been alone," I said. "Mum and Dad have insisted you come with me to their house for Christmas. I was going to ask you about it today, but..." I trailed off, shrugging.

My parents knew June from when they'd been to visit me and we'd been chatting on our doorsteps, or when June had been at my house. We'd all grown fond of her and none of us could stand the idea of her being on her own at Christmas just months after she'd lost her husband.

I'd been kind of looking forward to taking her to my family home, but being with her own family would be better for her.

June's hand rested on top of mine. "That's a lovely offer. One I would have taken you up on if Donovan wasn't here." She giggled. "I might just take you up on it anyway. For a twenty-eight-year-old, he's like a grumpy old man."

Her words made me laugh. Maybe I shouldn't have judged him on our tiny interaction, but he hadn't made a great first impression with his glare and bad attitude.

"Anyway, enough about that," June said, sipping her tea. "Tell me how your day went."

I launched into an explanation of my Friday at work. Seeing eight-year-olds getting excited for Christmas was delightful. The last couple of weeks of term were all about rehearsals for Christmas plays and making fun things the kids could take home to their parents.

The sound of the doorbell interrupted the conversation, and June carefully lifted herself from her seat.

"That'll be Donovan with the cream."

Oh, joy.

CHAPTER 2

DONOVAN

MY HOMETOWN WAS BOTH DIFFERENT YET SOMEHOW HADN'T CHANGED A bit. While many shops were new, the centre of town—The Lawn, the bandstand, the stream—had remained unchanged since my last visit.

Being back in the UK was strange. Like I'd stepped into another world or something. It was home, but it hadn't been for over fifteen years. Seeing familiar things made the transition easier, but I still felt detached somehow.

I had planned to return to the UK for more than a year, but there was always 'one more trip'. One more place to see. However, since my grandad had died, the trip I'd had most experience with was the guilt trip. My parents were appalled that I didn't come back for Grandad's funeral. The truth was, I hadn't wanted to face it. I had guilt enough about not seeing them in so long. I didn't want the first time I saw my grandma to be under those circumstances.

However, this would be her first Christmas alone. The circumstances weren't much better now, not when it was the season when everything was supposed to be happy. I'd long grown out of excitement about Christmas, but being with Nan when she was still mourning was going to make it rough and depressing, especially when I could have been sunning myself on a beach somewhere.

I'd made my living for the last seven years as a travel writer, and my blog, Off The Beaten Track, had gained popularity, allowing me to make money to keep globetrotting. Apparently, sarcasm, photography skills, and a couple of viral TikTok videos can take a person far. More followers meant more money, and I could have very easily afforded to buy my own home anywhere I wanted. However, I did *not* want the UK.

I picked up the clotted cream, already practically tasting it on my tongue as I drove back to my nan's house. I didn't have a key yet. I'd only arrived a few hours ago, so I rang the doorbell and waited for Nan to let me in. When she opened the door, she said, "I thought you'd got lost!"

I bristled slightly. I wasn't sure if that was a dig about me not staying in touch or visiting.

And, of course, you would only know whether or not it was a dig if you'd taken the time to stay in touch with her. I shook the thought away.

"It would be pretty hard to get lost in Dawlish. I was just having a look around," I told her as she let me inside.

She ushered me towards the kitchen, and I placed the carrier bag with two large pots of clotted cream inside down on the kitchen table.

"Can you pop the kettle on for me?" Nan asked as she reached into the cupboard and pulled out a box of mince pies. "Then fetch the cups from the living room."

That was when I remembered Nan's guest. The petite woman with unkempt light brown hair who had been on the doorstep just as I was leaving. She was short and curvy, but a little serious-looking, like a librarian.

"Is your friend still here?" I asked.

Nan smiled. "Yes. She always comes over on a Friday afternoon for tea and cakes."

"And who is she?"

"She lives next door at number thirty-five." Nan put a couple of mince pies on a plate and put them in the microwave. "She's been very kind to me since your grandad died."

I raised an eyebrow. "Are you sure she doesn't want anything from you?" I didn't know my nan as well as I should have, and I wasn't sure if she would be able to distinguish between a good neighbour and someone who was trying to take advantage of her. It wouldn't have been the first time someone tried to con an old lady out of their things by pretending to be a friend.

"I can assure you, the only thing I come here for is the company and to help your nan if she needs it."

Nan and I turned towards the cold voice from the living room doorway. The hurt flickering in her brown eyes filled me with discomfort, but how was I to know what she was up to? Scammers were everywhere these days, eager to take advantage. Perhaps her hurt look was simply the mark of an excellent actress.

Yeah, keep telling yourself that. Twat.

"Donovan," Nan said abruptly. "I don't know what kind of fool you think I am, but I know a decent person when I see one. And since we're on the topic of people wanting things, what did *you* come back for?"

Nan's hard glare made me feel like I was five years old again and about to be sent to sit on the stairs to think about what I'd just said.

The atmosphere in the room grew uncomfortable because, although we had talked since I arrived back, it hadn't been a long conversation, and it wasn't about why I was there. I wished I could say I was being the perfect, caring grandson, but that wouldn't have been the truth. It wasn't that I didn't love my nan and didn't want to see her, I'd just outgrown small-town life and would have preferred to spend the season somewhere hot instead of freezing my nuts off in England.

"Maybe I should go," the woman said, taking a small step backwards. "Thank you for the tea, but you two obviously have things you need to talk about."

"No," Nan said, shooting another glare at me. "Please. My grandson spoke out of turn." As if on cue, the microwave pinged, telling us the first two mince pies were done.

"I'll leave you to it," I said. "I'm going for a walk. I'll be back later."

Before anyone could protest, I squeezed my large frame around Nan's neighbour and headed back outside.

CHAPTER 3

NOVA

I stood in stunned silence as Donovan shuffled past me and out the front door he'd only just entered through.

June pulled the mince pies from the microwave and set them down on the counter with a sigh.

"Are you okay?" I asked, unsure what to say for the best. Was I the one who caused that argument? Maybe I should have pretended I didn't hear what Donovan said, but it pissed me off that the immediate assumption he'd made about me was that I was trying to rip off his grandmother. He might have been good-looking, but his attitude was shitty.

June pushed the plate towards me and gestured to the clotted cream on the table. "I'm fine, love. I didn't mean to snap at him, but I won't hear of anyone accusing you of anything untoward."

I offered her an understanding smile as I reached into the drawer to grab a couple of spoons for us.

"Hasn't he explained why he's here?" I asked, taking a seat at the table and pulling the tops off the mince pies, ready to spoon the cream into them. I winced when the hot pastry burned my fingertips.

"Not yet." June put another couple of mince pies onto a plate and into the microwave. "But I think guilt has a lot to do with it." She sighed again. "I don't blame him for not visiting more. He was busy having his own life. It did hurt that he didn't come to Trevor's funeral, but again, why would he? Donovan didn't really know him." She moved around to the kettle to flick the switch. "I didn't mean to suggest he was after anything by coming here, but what do I know about him now?"

The confusion on her face made me stand up and go to her. She was far from some weak old lady who could be tricked, but I could kind of understand why she questioned what Donovan might want from her. After all, he had projected deception at me right away. Why would that have been his first thought if *he* wasn't looking to gain something from his grandmother?

Or maybe you know nothing about him and he's jet-lagged and grouchy. I hadn't had long enough to get any kind of read on him, so I couldn't judge.

"I think you two need to talk," I said, giving her a hug and then walking her over to sit down at the table. "It's kind of unrealistic to expect the two of you to just bond immediately after being apart for so long. I mean... when was the last time you even spoke to each other?"

June shook her head as she thought it over. "I think he called me after Trevor died. I can't remember what we talked about because my mind was all over the place. And before that... probably Christmas. He did always phone us at Christmas."

I grabbed the mince pies out of the microwave because I could hear them starting to bubble. "I guess you need to reconnect."

"If he'll forgive me for what I said to him." She looked up at me as I handed her pies over. "This has just been a big shock. Perhaps I'll ring his parents and see if they know anything more about why he came here."

We tucked into our Christmas treats, swiftly changing the subject to more pleasant things like the weekend Christmas market we were planning to go to on Sunday. June had been going with Trevor for as long as the Christmas market had been running, and I'd promised to go with her this year, so she wasn't alone.

Unless Donovan had something to say about that too.

I STAYED WITH JUNE FOR ANOTHER HOUR BEFORE HEADING HOME TO order myself a pizza and relax. The TV was on in the background as I sat beside my white light-lit Christmas tree. A ripple of giddy joy shot through me knowing Christmas was on its way. I had no plans for the following day, which meant a lie-in, followed by a totally lazy day. Sunday was market day, and then it was fun stuff at school before the holidays. Although there was still plenty of work to do, it somehow felt better with carols echoing down the hallways and festive displays in the classrooms—many of which I had a hand in.

The doorbell sounded, breaking me from my glee-filled trance. I'd long since finished my pizza, and very rarely did anyone visit unannounced. It was just past eight p.m., which wasn't late, but probably too late for anyone trying to sell me something. I glanced down at my super sexy Marvel pjs, hoping it wasn't anyone important.

Getting off the sofa, I went to the door, flicking on the hall light. Through the frosted glass at the top of the door, the outline of a head was visible, but that didn't tell me much.

I opened the door a fraction, peering around the frame. My jaw nearly unhinged when I saw Donovan standing there, hands in his pockets, shuffling from foot to foot. I wasn't sure if it was from the cold or because… well, I had no idea.

"Hi," I said, unable to disguise the hint of incredulity in my voice. I kept myself partially shielded behind the door as I wasn't sure whether he was here to be friendly or was about to accuse me of something else I had no intention of doing.

"Hi." An awkward expression somewhere between a smile and a grimace crossed his face. "I owe you an apology." My eyebrows rose, but before I could say anything, he added, "I've been driving around, trying to get my head straight for hours. I haven't even been back to my nan's yet."

I could feel my brows creeping higher up my forehead. He must have done some serious soul-searching to visit me before going home.

"I'm sorry for taking my frustration with myself out on you," he continued, pushing his hands further into his jacket pockets. The denim wasn't nearly enough to protect him from the icy chill outside that was beginning to creep into my house. "It wasn't your fault, and I should have kept my mouth shut."

Whether it was the Christmas spirit I'd been basking in or something else, a rush of empathy for him washed over me. He looked so uncomfortable standing there, not to mention he was puffing out little clouds of cold breath into the air.

"Do you want to come in?" I asked, opening the door a little wider and instantly regretting it when the cold breeze blew right inside.

"Erm... yeah. Sure."

As he stepped inside, I felt like an idiot. *Why the hell did you say that? What else is left to say now he's apologised?* But for whatever reason, I *had* said it, and now we were both standing awkwardly in my hallway.

I noticed him looking at my attire and couldn't help laughing, running my hands through my hair and pushing it back out of my face. "Yeah, I wasn't really expecting anyone to stop by."

Donovan chuckled and, for just a moment, a chink appeared in his frosty armour. His smile was slightly lopsided and caused his eyes to crinkle at the corners and the blue of his irises to sparkle. "I'm sorry. I just... I wanted to clear the air." His face grew serious again. "Not that it's any excuse, but I only got to the UK yesterday after travelling for forty-eight hours, and even though I'm knackered, I'm too wired to sleep. It's making me say stuff without thinking it through."

Now I was getting the chance to look at him properly, I could see a hint of the dark circles under his eyes, and he ran a hand through his hair.

"Apology accepted," I told him. "Let's just start over. Do you want a drink?"

He hesitated for a moment, opening his mouth as if to decline, but then he said, "Yeah. That would be great, thanks."

CHAPTER 4

DONOVAN

Perhaps it was pity that made her invite me in for a drink. I was exhausted and probably looked pathetic, but I'd wanted to apologise for what I'd said to her earlier, and I didn't want it hanging over me all night. The last thing I needed was something else to feel bad about. I wasn't sure what my excuse was for agreeing to a drink, though. Since I'd pissed her off on our first meeting, I didn't imagine she'd have much to say to me, unless my nan had given her some ammunition; I had no idea what was said about me after I left.

Still, she was cute, even in her pyjamas. Too bad she was already pre-prepared to dislike me.

Nan's neighbour—whose name I hadn't got yet—made each of us a mug of hot chocolate with marshmallows; something I hadn't had in years. While it was a little juvenile, I was just grateful she hadn't thrown it at me.

She led me through to her living room, which was decorated with simple frosted pink and silver baubles on her tree, and a few pale pink hanging ceiling decorations. Very nineties retro. The room's warmth shrouded us, some of the lingering chill dissipating as we sat down. We situated ourselves at opposite ends of her sofa, and a slight awkwardness descended over the room.

"So," she began. "What are your plans for the next few weeks?"

I raised an eyebrow, surprised she hadn't pushed more about why I was less than pleasant to her earlier. She *had* said we should start over, but even so... I'd expected her to want some kind of explanation for my attitude.

"Well," I said with a sigh, "I think I'm going to try and sleep through tomorrow so I'm not such a prick."

Her lips curved into a small grin, but she didn't say anything.

"Then, I'll figure out where I'm going next."

"Oh. Are you not sticking around for long?"

I shook my head. "Nope. I'll be gone the day after Boxing Day. Things to see. Places to write about." When she raised a questioning eyebrow, I said, "I'm a travel writer. I started a blog seven years ago, and now it's how I make a living."

"Impressive," she said, and her expression suggested she wasn't just mocking me. Believe me, if I'd heard what I'd just said, I would have laughed. Friendliness wasn't exactly my strong suit. I definitely wasn't the kind of sunny internet personality needed to make it big. I'd gained readers and followers after a rant I'd had about some toilets in a pub that were so dirty I needed to call it out. My British phrasing and obvious disgust had amused people, and since then, I was branded 'honest and refreshing'. The more honest I was, the more people jumped on my bandwagon. "What's the name of the blog?"

"Off The Beaten Track." The words came out with a slight cringe that didn't go unnoticed.

"What was that look for?" she asked, laughing.

The sound seemed to travel through my body, easing some of my tension, and I rolled my shoulders. "I mean... you've met me." I smiled a little sheepishly. "I'm not exactly obvious influencer material."

She pulled her lips together as if trying to suppress another laugh. "You might have a point there. But even so, you're doing well by the sounds of it."

"I am. I love what I do and I'm proud I can earn a living from it, but it wasn't what I expected to be doing with my life. Sometimes, when I tell people I make my money by writing reviews and guides to places I've been, they usually roll their eyes, like I'm just another one of *those* people dossing around and doing nothing with their life."

Also, they're probably right. Not that my writing and photography weren't decent. It had hopefully stopped a few people wandering into dodgy areas of certain cities and told them the best places to eat or sightsee in others. But a part of me rebelled against 'growing up'. With a whole world to explore, why settle down?

Her eyes softened a little, the humour dialling down. "Whatever you're doing, it's working for you. Any ideas where you'll go next?"

"Not yet. All I know is I can't stay with Nan forever. I think she already wants to smother me with a pillow."

She laughed out loud. "June would never do that. You're her grandson. She just needs to get to know you again."

Letting out a slow breath, I said, "Yeah, maybe. Speaking of getting to know people... I haven't been told your name yet."

Her eyes widened, her cheeks colouring slightly. "Oh, God. I'm so sorry. I'm Nova."

Nova.

Where the hell did I know that name from? It wasn't common, but I'd definitely heard it before. The sound of it was tickling a distant corner of my mind.

"Are you okay?" she asked, her forehead crinkling as she looked at me. Clearly, my confusion was showing on my face.

Nodding, I said, "Yeah, I'm just... your name sounds familiar, but I can't work out why since I didn't grow up around here. If I had, we would probably have gone to the same school."

"Your nan said you're twenty-eight, and I'm twenty-six, so yeah, we would have. But I don't know the name Donovan, so I guess you must have heard my name somewhere else."

I nodded again, more slowly as I searched the depths of my memory. Not Australia, not New Zealand. Longer ago than even my first trip overseas. A school friend in Italy? I had a pretty decent memory for names and faces, and I couldn't recall anyone with that name being around me for a substantial amount of time.

A holiday maybe?

And then it hit me.

"No fucking way."

Again, her brows furrowed. I must have looked like an idiot drifting off into my thoughts like that, but I couldn't make sense of what I was remembering. Looking more closely at her, I could see it. Her eyes were a deeper brown, her hair a little darker and much thicker and longer, but I *knew* her.

"Nova McKay," I said.

She tilted her head to the side. "You know me?"

A laugh escaped my lips as I took in her heart-shaped face, full of questions and confusion. "Picture me about three foot shorter, no beard, my hair spiked up with gel like I was in a nineties boyband."

Nova stared at me like she was trawling her mind for answers, but there was still no recognition coming through yet.

"When I was a kid, my grandad lived next door to you and your parents," I said. "I came with my mum and dad to stay with him for two Christmases. When we came back the third year, Grandad said you'd gone to live in Exeter."

For a moment, I was swept back to the day I found out my Christmas holiday friend had moved away. I was eleven, and even though Nova was two years younger than me, I'd got used to spending the festive season with her. She would come into my grandad's house and my mum would set up art projects for us to play with, or I'd go into her house and we'd bake cookies with her mum. We'd all gone ice skating in Plymouth together once, and both Christmases, we'd created some traditions I'd expected to carry on for at least a few more years.

Her eyes widened, and her hands flew up to cover her mouth. "You? That little boy I played with during the Christmas holidays was you?"

I nodded. "I wasn't sure you'd remember. You must have only been eight the last time we saw each other."

"Oh my God." She burst out laughing, her smile wide. The memories must have helped soften her towards me, and she leaned forward and rested her hand on my leg. "Of course I remember! The first Christmas after we moved, I begged Mum and Dad to bring me back to Dawlish to see you, but we couldn't because we were going on holiday, and then after that, we heard your grandad had died." A frown crossed her face for a moment, and the mood dipped.

The death of my grandfather on my dad's side was the first I'd experienced, and it symbolised an end to the innocence of childhood. My paternal grandmother had died when I was too young to remember her, although my grandad and my dad told me all about her.

"Nobody ever called you Donovan," she said. "You were Donnie back then. Mum said you were probably called Donald! Donnie seemed better." She giggled.

I winced. "Yeah. Nobody calls me Donnie anymore. I refused to answer to it when I started secondary school."

"How crazy is it that I've managed to live next door to both sets of your grandparents," Nova said, shaking her head as she leaned back against the sofa and picked up her drink.

I shrugged. "Small town. Everyone knows each other in a small town."

She must have detected the hint of distaste in my words as her smile faded a little. "Yeah. I suppose so."

I could almost see her struggling over whether to ask any questions, and she picked off a couple of marshmallows from her drink and popped them into her mouth.

"What made you move back to Dawlish?" I asked, trying not to sound like I was judging her for remaining local.

A hint must have slipped into my tone, as she licked her lower lip before answering as if she were considering biting it to keep her true thoughts from spilling out. "I love this town. The seaside, the people. I still work in Exeter, but Dawlish will always be home."

"What do you do?"

"I teach at a primary school."

That explained her modest dress sense from earlier. "Are your parents still in Exeter?"

"Yeah." She let out a small laugh. "My mum isn't going to believe

I've met you again." A contemplative look crossed her face before she smiled again. "Your parents still live in Italy, right?"

"Yeah. Tuscany. It's beautiful over there. I'll go and visit them for a week or two after I leave here." Even though I'd spent my teenage years there, it never fully felt like home. Probably because I'd spent parts of my childhood in several different places. A long-term ex of mine cited that as my reason for being unwilling to commit to her. My 'unstable' childhood. It wasn't really unstable, though; just a bit shaky until my parents chose a place to put down some roots.

"Your parents were lovely," Nova said, smiling. "Your mum was always so much fun."

"She hasn't changed much."

After taking another sip of her drink, Nova said, "I'm sad I didn't know the connection sooner. At your grandad's funeral, I sat way back so as not to intrude, and the wake was family only, so I didn't meet them. And, of course, knowing someone was with June, I kept out of the way so they could grieve together. I don't think I even saw them while they were here."

"Yeah. My mum took Grandad's death really hard. They wanted to stay for longer, but Dad had to get back home for work."

Nova nodded. "Your nan said she wished they'd been able to stay, but she understood. She has friends here, which helps, though."

"And you, apparently." I offered her a smile. "Thanks for taking care of her. I appreciate it."

"It's what we do around here." She paused, gazing at me for a moment. "It's not my place, but could I offer a piece of advice?"

A pit of dread opened up in my stomach. We may have had some kind of childhood connection, and I'd conceded she was a decent person, but I wasn't sure I wanted advice from an almost stranger. Still, I wasn't totally sure I knew what the hell I was doing or how to talk to my nan after so long, so I nodded.

"When you go back to your nan, be honest with her," Nova said. "If you have things you want to tell her, do it. She loves you very much, so be real with her." Pausing, she grinned, sitting up straighter. "Come with us to the Christmas market on Sunday."

I couldn't remember the last time I'd been to a Christmas market. Must have been at least five years ago, when I was in Germany.

"I don't know," I said with a sigh. "I don't want to intrude on any more of your traditions like I did today. I don't much care for Christmas since Santa stopped coming."

She raised an eyebrow. "Maybe he'd come if you weren't such a grump."

For a moment, I wanted to tell her to mind her own damn business and stop judging me, but I'd done the same to her on our first meeting too. Plus, it was hard to be pissed off with her when she looked so fucking cute sitting there in her PJs with her hot chocolate, and her hair falling around her face.

"I'll come to the market," I said. "But I'm not participating in singing carols or wearing a Christmas jumper."

"That's fair." She smiled triumphantly. "But I fully expect you to smile at least once during the day."

"Is that a hard condition of me coming along?" My brow furrowed, and she laughed.

"I'm afraid so!"

With a dramatic sigh, even though I was only kidding, I said, "Fine. But you're buying the mulled wine."

CHAPTER 5

NOVA

"IS THERE ANYTHING MORE FESTIVE THAN THIS?" I SAID, MY ARM LINKED through June's as we began our walk down The Strand, the main street of Dawlish town centre.

Usually, the road was a line of slow-moving traffic, but for market day, it was closed and numerous stalls lined the street on both sides. In typical Christmas market weekend fashion, the weather was icy and the wind was whipping around, occasionally making traders' wares wobble or fall over on their tables. Everyone was wrapped up in thick winter coats, sturdy boots, scarves, hats, and gloves, but the weather never dampened the spirits of the locals. Christmas songs blasted from an invisible speaker, and some of the people danced as they walked by or browsed the stalls. The Christmas lights on the lampposts illuminated the dark day, adding to the cheer.

"I think we need to find the nearest hot drinks stall and warm up," June said with a laugh, shuffling a little closer to me, but there was a bright smile on her face.

Donovan trailed behind us, wearing a bigger coat than the denim jacket he'd worn when I met him. It was long, thick, and black—not entirely dissimilar to my own. A deep blue scarf was around his neck, blue jeans covered his legs, and he had brown Timberland boots on his feet.

"We can do that," I said as we reached the first stall, which offered an array of handmade scented candles and wax melts.

June scrunched up her nose. "They're a bit strong for me," she said as the combining scents wafted in the air.

"Ooh, I don't know," I said, reaching for a pale pink candle labelled Winter Rose. I brought it to my nose and breathed in deeply, closing my eyes. "That's gorgeous."

The stall owner, a blonde-haired lady with sparkly green eyes, grinned. "That's my favourite."

"Can I have two, please?" I asked, inhaling another whiff. I knew my mum would love it as much as I did, and it was another small Christmas gift I could cross off my list.

"You know this is only the first stall, don't you?" Donovan said over my shoulder, and I whipped my head around to look at him. He was slightly leaning over me to peer at the candles, then he turned his attention back to me with a smirk on his face.

"And?"

"What if there's another stall further down with even better candles?"

I shrugged a shoulder. "You can never have too many candles."

He rolled his eyes, and June gave him a light slap on the arm. "Leave her be," she said while I turned back around to pay for my treats.

Once they had been wrapped and put in a bag, I thanked the trader and we continued our stroll.

The scents all around were making my mouth water. The aroma of mulled wine floated towards us, but I could also smell burgers and sausages cooking from a catering van brought along by a local farmer. I knew even more goodies would be available further on, so I tried to ignore the groan in my stomach until I knew for sure what I wanted.

"Are you looking for anything today?" I asked June, as Donovan walked beside her.

"No, not really," she said, casting her eyes towards The Strand

Centre, which was set in what was formerly the United Reformed Church. A small choir seemed to be preparing to sing some carols outside. "I give everyone money these days because nobody ever knows what they want."

"And what do you want for Christmas, Donovan?" I asked, looking at him over June's head.

A healthy dose of Christmas spirit? A bit of enthusiasm for spending time with your grandmother? Those were things he probably didn't want but definitely needed.

I hadn't seen him again after he left my house on Friday evening, but June said he hadn't spoken to her much on Saturday. He'd mostly slept, and he obviously hadn't taken my advice to open up to her. Part of me had some empathy for how awkward it must have been to be around a family member he had hardly had any contact with for years, but he could have made more effort. Thinking about it, June and Trevor could have reached out to him too, but from what I'd heard, they *had* tried when he'd first gone travelling. However, with him on the move so much, it had become very hard for them to know where he was. June said he rarely replied to the emails they sent him, so in the end, they just stopped.

I still hadn't wrapped my head around the fact that he was the little boy I played with for two Christmases. His youthful joy did not match the somewhat frosty man he'd grown into. Surely, someone who travelled for a living should be a lot more light-hearted. All I got from him now was the impression he didn't really want to be here.

I'd called my mum to tell her about the unexpected reunion, and she was stunned too. She didn't understand how she could have not known about the connection between Donovan's two sets of grandparents. When she'd asked what he looked like now, I'd hesitated. For all his attitude, he *was* good-looking, and I didn't lie about it. But I'd also made it very clear *I* wasn't really attracted to him. Had I met him as a random in a bar, I'd probably have been interested, but because of how we had bumped into each other, his looks weren't quite enough to make him appealing.

Donovan glanced down at me, frowning at the teasing grin on my face. I couldn't help myself, though. His cynical mood was killing my buzz.

"A Christmas dinner with pigs in blankets, and a nap in front of the King's speech."

"Don't you want an actual gift?" I asked.

Donovan shook his head, his scarf slipping with the movement. "I've lived mostly out of a suitcase for ten years. I don't need anything material."

"You can't live out of a suitcase forever, Donovan," June said, turning to him. I guided us towards another stall that intrigued me, this one covered with handmade necklaces, bracelets, rings, and earrings.

"Why not?" he asked. "Moving around means I don't ever have to get bored."

"It also means you'll never have the chance to know what it's like to be content in one place. Have a community. A family."

Something mischievous I'd never seen before flashed across his face, and I wondered what it was for. Withheld sarcasm, maybe? "Nan, I've had a lot of communities and a lot of families in the places I've been."

"Yes, but where are they now? Where will they be when you need a friend? When you want to start your own family?"

I kept my eyes trained on the sparkly jewellery in front of me, but I could just imagine June's lips set in a firm line. There was a low ripple of resentment running from her to Donovan. I desperately wanted to interrupt, to change the subject, but this conversation wasn't my business.

I picked up a box containing a pair of earrings shaped like snowflakes with a tiny silver stone in the centre. *Maybe if I stuff these in my ears, I'll be able to block out what they're saying.*

"I'm happy as I am, Nan," Donovan said. "Now is not the time for this conversation."

Subtly, I gave June's arm a squeeze with mine, letting her know I was there for her, even if I wasn't meant to be listening.

June let out a long sigh. "You're right, but that doesn't mean this is over."

I placed the earrings back down, thinking I would come back for them later, and said, "Why don't we get those drinks?"

With a smile, June said, "If you don't mind, I'm just going to pop back to The Strand Centre and listen to the carol singers. I'll catch you up in a bit."

I nodded, understanding she needed a breather from Donovan, even though we'd only been out for less than an hour. Still, she lived with him, so maybe she was hoping for a bit of space to clear her head.

Still in front of the jewellery stall, I looked up at Donovan. "Well, that was handled nicely." Sarcasm dripped from my words, and Donovan took me by the elbow and led me back into the middle of the street.

"What did you want me to say to her?" he asked as we carefully weaved in and out of other shoppers. "I like my lifestyle."

"I'm sure you do, but is it really something you want to do forever?"

"Who knows?" He shrugged. "But let me ask you this. Are you honestly saying you think it's okay to ask someone if they plan to start a family? These days, that is not exactly appropriate."

I stopped walking, edging us sideways out of the way of people before looking up at him again. His blue eyes held a challenge. "While I agree that question is inappropriate, that wasn't what she said."

"But she was the one who started that conversation."

"Maybe because she wants to know your plans. Have you even talked to her yet?"

The coldness in the air was rapidly overtaken by the look in Donovan's eyes. "Look, you and I might have been friends once, but you don't know me now. It's not your place to tell me what I need to do about my own grandmother."

My eyebrow rose at his tone. A scathing response sat on the tip of my tongue, but I'd heard the undertone of guilt laced subtly through his words. That fact halted the rant that had threatened to spill from my lips, because he was right. No matter how much of a closed-off pain in the ass he had been so far, I didn't know him anymore, and it *was* June who had set off that line of conversation.

The hunch of his shoulders wasn't only to protect him from the wind and chill, and my temper settled. Donovan wasn't as unfeeling as he'd first appeared to be; he was affected by the icy exchange with his nan, and I didn't want to spend the rest of the morning with us sniping at each other.

Heaving in a breath, I said, "Okay, fine. You handle things however you want to. But please don't forget she's still grieving."

"Do you think I'm not?"

Considering he hadn't made the effort to come back for the funeral, I wasn't sure I knew the answer.

I guess he could be grieving for everything he missed out on.

Shaking my head because I had no intention of trying to second guess anything he was thinking, I sighed again. "I'm sure you are, but she lost the man she spent over fifty years with. And she's facing her first Christmas without him, so cut her a little slack."

He gave an almost imperceptible nod, and then we began walking again, the Christmas music still loud and the scent of mulled wine getting stronger.

"Do you want a drink?" I asked him as we approached the wine stall.

"Yeah, why not? Can I interest you in a mince pie and some cream?"

I glanced at him sideways, and he was almost smiling, our heated words already brushed aside.

"I'm always interested in a mince pie."

Donovan chuckled. "Me too."

I paid for a cup of mulled wine for each of us, and Donovan went to the next stall along for our food. He came back carrying two paper plates, each with a mince pie and a generous helping of clotted cream on top, and two plastic forks. We locked eyes, trying to work out how to swap a cup and a plate each with our hands full, and I said, "Let's go and sit down somewhere."

We walked to the end of the street, then turned right onto The

Lawn, which had a path running alongside it with some benches dotted at various intervals. With it being so cold, not many people were sitting, so it didn't take us long to find a vacant seat.

Once we sat, we rested our treats down, and I instantly reached for the mulled wine to warm up my hands through my thin gloves. Conversely, Donovan went for the food first, pushing his fork into the pastry and cream before taking a bite.

He closed his eyes as he swallowed, as if savouring the taste, and I laughed before taking a drink of the wine. "I'm almost positive you didn't like mince pies as a kid."

Donovan smiled. "I didn't. But after many years of not having them, I decided to try them again when I was back in Italy with my parents, and I wondered why I ever hated them."

"What was it like?" I asked. "I mean… Christmases in different countries. It must have been strange, especially in Australia."

"Yeah. My first Christmas in Australia was weird. Seeing people on the beach on Christmas Day and not having to be wrapped up in big jumpers was a shock to my system. But I've also spent Christmases in the Philippines and Thailand. And also a Thanksgiving and Christmas in Wisconsin."

My eyes widened. "Why Wisconsin?"

"I like true crime documentaries. I was one of those people who got swept up in *Making a Murderer*, and I was in Chicago when I watched it. So, I decided to swing over to Manitowoc County."

"Oh my God," I said, staring at him, amazed we might have something in common. "I love true crime documentaries. What was it like there?"

He told me a little about his experiences in Wisconsin, and I couldn't stop looking at him as he spoke with such passion about his travels and what Thanksgiving was like. I decided I would look up his blog when I got home because if his writing was as passionate as his conversation, it was no surprise he was so popular.

"What?" he asked, and I realised I was staring at him.

Shaking my head, I said, "Sorry. I just… the way you talk about the things you've done. It's really interesting. Maybe you should write a book."

"I've considered it, but I don't think I have much to say that I haven't already said on my blog. Plus, I don't know if I want people to know too much about my real experiences. I give away a lot to my readers, but it's mostly surface stuff. Thoughts on places, but not as much about how I felt when I was there. Nothing about people I met or had friendships or relationships with. That's just for me. Or for those I choose to tell."

He was such a contradiction. Grumpy on the outside, but I'd seen flickers of emotion showing through occasionally. He was private, but he shared his travels. He was not totally happy about being in the UK, but he didn't seem to have a really big problem with nostalgia because he liked talking about the things he'd done.

"Nova, you're staring again."

Heat flushed across my cheeks, and I laughed, seeing his smile. "Sorry… again. You have so many stories you could share. It's mind-blowing to me."

"Well, which countries have you been to?"

My answer was embarrassing compared to how many places he'd been to. "My parents and I went to Spain a few times when I was little. Barcelona, to be precise. Then I went to Greece before I started university with some friends, and to Paris after uni with a boyfriend."

"Well, you've been to one country I haven't been to. I haven't got to Greece yet. It's on the list." He paused, taking a final drink of his wine. "What's on your list?"

I shrugged. "Never really thought about it. I guess I've always wanted to go to Italy. I'd like to see Rome."

Donovan placed his empty cup on top of his now discarded plate. "Well, why don't you?"

"Time. Money. Also, who would I go with? It doesn't seem like it would be much fun alone."

"I've been mostly doing it on my own since I left. I did spend three years with one girl, but… it didn't work out."

Nothing in his expression said he was sad about their break-up, but I wasn't sure how long ago that had been. It struck me as strange that he had spent so long with one person, but there were still seven years when he was on his own. Didn't he miss the company?

"Wasn't it better when you had someone to share it all with, though?" I asked.

Another pause. "Not better. Just different. It was fun to talk about all the things we'd seen together. All the romantic walks along beaches and stuff. But without her, I got to meet a lot of other people. When I was with Paige, I met a lot less people. Even fewer who I stayed in touch with once we moved on. Being alone, I got to know others who were passing through, locals in bars, and business owners. All kinds of people, because nobody but me decided what to do with my time."

Maybe he'd been alone for too long now. My grandad died when I was twelve, and after a few years of him being gone, I asked my grandma if she wanted to meet someone new. She laughed and said she was too set in her ways. But Donovan was much younger than her. Perhaps it wasn't about being used to being on his own, just that he kept himself so busy he didn't have a second to think about it.

"Are you really close to any of the people you met? Like, call them up when you're having a bad day kind of close?"

"I have my parents for that. But I do have close friends still in Australia and New Zealand. I spent a lot of time in Sydney and Auckland." His eyes grew distant, wistful, as if wishing he were back in one of those places. "But you've changed the subject. We were talking about where you want to go."

Shrugging again, I said, "I guess I'm just a person who likes her home comforts."

Again, a small hint of judgement crossed his face, wobbling the foundations of friendship we were somehow rebuilding. Everything was simpler when we were kids. Just two children enjoying the best season. Now, he was in town under duress and didn't even like Christmas—food and drink aside—much. He'd experienced so much that small-town life was unappealing, and I'd experienced so little that breaking out of my 'normal' seemed alien.

But I *liked* my life. Liked where I lived, and the community. A holiday would have been nice, but I had a beach right on my doorstep. Okay, it was cold and rainy a lot of the time, but it was still beautiful. In fact, wandering down to Coryton Cove—the secret beach that not all tourists knew about—was my happy place. I loved to sit outside the Cove Café in the summer with a cold drink and a slice of cake, just looking out at the sea.

"Well, if you ever change your mind, I'll gladly give you some recommendations," Donovan said.

I offered him a small smile, then said, "We should go and look for your nan."

"Yeah, we should."

After clearing away our rubbish, we wandered down the much less busy path beside The Lawn, then back up to The Strand Centre, where June was still happily watching the carol singers. They were pretty decent and had drawn a crowd. However, something about my conversation with Donovan had dimmed my mood. Maybe it was because I suddenly wondered if I'd been missing out by dedicating my life to work and family, or maybe I just didn't appreciate the judgemental glances he sometimes threw my way.

Whatever it was, I simply didn't enjoy the market as much as I usually did.

When I got home, I snuggled up on the sofa under a blanket with a cup of coffee and watched Christmas movies to restore my faith in the festive season. It wasn't until the evening that I decided to look up Donovan's blog. Curiosity had plagued me all afternoon, but I didn't *want* to be interested in where he'd been. I'd tried to keep away from it, but for some reason, I was desperate to understand why he was the way he was.

His blog exuded professionalism, and a small photo of Donovan sat in the top left-hand corner. Even in his picture, he still looked somewhat grumpy. But he had said that was a part of his online persona. It was kinda hard to know what was real and what wasn't with him sometimes. It was still messing with my brain to think about how joyful he was as a child compared to now. My love of Christmas hadn't dwindled. At all. Maybe that was part of the appeal of teaching.

It meant I still got to get swept up in that giddy excitement children have as December comes around.

As my eyes glanced down the blog page, I noticed a brand new post, submitted a couple of hours ago. Shortly after we'd returned home from the market. The bold white headline read: Hometown Blues. *Hmm, not a positive start.*

Intrigued, I clicked to read more.

You may or may not know this, but as a child, I spent a lot of my time in Devon, in the UK. I hadn't been there in years, and returning has thrown up a lot of curiosity about life within a small community. Today, I experienced Dawlish Christmas Market again. It was just how I remembered it to be. Lots of locals enjoying the music and the atmosphere. Stalls selling Christmas gifts and delicious treats. If you like that kind of thing, I'd highly recommend a visit.

But the thing is, a small part of me hoped I'd feel... something. Don't get me wrong, I love the nostalgia of my family's hometown. So many things are the same or similar. But I just don't know how I could settle in a place where everyone is so close-knit. In a way, it's nice, but in another way, it makes me feel shut in.

I hoped being around something familiar would re-ignite 'the magic of Christmas'. That hasn't happened so far, and I'm coming around to the fact that Christmas is just not as much fun as an adult. Not that I hadn't figured it out years ago. It was more of a confirmation that I've lost something I can't get back.

Even so, Dawlish is a great town. I just don't think there is anything here for me now.

As I finished reading, several thoughts hit me at once. The teacher in me wanted to give him a C for effort. I assumed more work went into other things he'd written because that was more of a self-indulgent whine about how he was bigger than the small town he visited when he was younger. Our hometown had plenty to offer. Nothing about it made me feel 'shut in'. If anything, knowing so many people gave me a sense of safety. I liked familiarity. I loved the tradition of the market and knowing what to expect from it. I loved carnival week, and summer fetes on The Lawn. I didn't deny there was a lot of world to explore, but this was where I would always come back to.

On the other hand, Donovan's expression of being too old for Christmas magic made me a little sad. Perhaps I might have understood if I'd done as much moving around in my life as he had. Because really, most of his childhood Christmases were split between somewhere in Cornwall, Dawlish, and then Italy.

What the hell had happened on his travels? What had made him cynical?

I closed down his blog page, but I held my phone in my hand as a strange idea began to form in my mind.

What if I could change that for him? What if I could make him view the Christmas spirit the way he used to? As an adult, it was all worry about the costs of buying gifts and stress over cooking the perfect Christmas lunch. Well, maybe not for him since he was never in one specific home, but even so, something was inherently missing from his view of the season these days.

Grabbing a notebook and pen from under my coffee table, I wrote *Re-Writing Christmas* at the top of the first page. I chuckled. He was the writer, and *I* was going to help *him* re-write his outlook. Hopefully.

Barely needing to think, I began writing, smiling to myself as snippets of well-buried memories pushed themselves to the surface of my mind.

When I was done, I read over everything I'd written, making sure it all looked right, then I ran upstairs to my tiny home office to grab an envelope. I put the note inside and scrawled *Donovan* on the envelope before running back downstairs and putting on my shoes. Since I was only going to be a second, I didn't bother with a coat, nor did I lock the door. I just opened it, rushed to June's place, then pushed the envelope through the letterbox. Not hanging around in case someone came quickly, I hurried back to my own house and shut the door, leaning against it to catch my breath from the speed of my sprint.

Operation Re-Writing Christmas was about to go live.

CHAPTER 6

DONOVAN

"Did something just come through the letterbox?" Nan asked, following a soft clicking sound from the hallway.

She and I were sitting in her living room, neither of us saying anything as the TV played in the background. I hadn't been listening; I was too busy catching up on some of my favourite blogs that I'd missed over the last few days.

"I'll go and check," I said, standing from the sofa.

"It's probably just junk mail."

I expected her to be right, so when I saw a white envelope on the brown doormat, I said, "Looks more like a Christmas card."

I reached down to pick it up, but right away, I could tell it wasn't a card unless it was one of those really flimsy ones. The envelope was way too light. I carried it back to the living room and handed it to Nan before sitting down again, continuing to look at my phone.

"This is for you," she said, offering it back in my direction.

My brow furrowed. "Me? Nobody knows I'm here." It wasn't as if I knew anyone who lived in town anymore, aside from my grandmother.

She seemed to be trying to conceal a grin, and I took the envelope from her and tore it open, pulling out the contents. Inside was a folded A5 piece of paper which had writing on both sides. I opened it up, and my eyes widened as I began to read.

Donovan,

I've just read your most recent blog post. I can't decide if you were trying to talk up this town or say it is somehow beneath you. However, I am going to give you the benefit of the doubt. For now.

I have a proposition for you. See, there was a time once, even though it was only short, that Christmas meant hanging out with you. My friend next door who came to visit. The way I see it, we're back where we started. You're here for the holidays. You're next door again. I don't know what the hell happened on your travels, but it seems to me you need a reminder of the good side of small-town life and an even bigger reminder of what Christmas is all about.

This is what I'm deeming our Christmas hit list. We have about two and a half weeks until Christmas. So, we're going to be kids again. We're going to revisit our old traditions and do things we used to enjoy. Take off your cynical adult head. Leave your judgements at the door. It's time to re-write Christmas.

I turned the page over and found a list written on the back.

1. Festive flashbacks
2. Slip not
3. Late night cruising
4. Keep it sweet
5. Judge me

If I told you what each of these things meant, I know you wouldn't even try. Admittedly, if I had more time, these 'clues' would be more imaginative, but I'm not the writer here. So, pick one that sounds appealing, and we'll give it a go. They *don't have to be done in order. Let me know if you accept this mission in the usual way.*

In the usual way.

Wow. I'd forgotten. When I stayed with my grandad before, Nova and I used to post letters through each other's letterboxes. It started when, after we'd met for the first time and played together, Nova's mum had said she could invite me over the next day, and she'd done so by posting a note through my grandad's door. I don't remember exactly what it said, but it was an invitation to go and play. My mum thought it was cute, and she told me to send a note back. For the whole week I stayed there, even if we'd been together most of the day, we would post letters back and forth until it got too dark to go outside.

"Why is Nova sending you letters?" Nan asked, and I looked over at her, still a little dazed by my trip down memory lane.

"What?" I asked, shaking my head.

She gestured towards the note in my hand. "I recognise her handwriting."

I hadn't told her about the connection between Nova and me yet. When I got back on Friday night from talking to her, I'd more or less said goodnight to my nan and gone to bed, then slept most of the next day. And although we'd been back from the market for a while, I'd spent some of that time writing my blog post in my room before joining Nan downstairs.

I placed the note down beside me on the sofa and said, "Do you remember when we used to come here for Christmas when I was younger to see Grandad Cain?"

Nan nodded. "I do. You used to come here first, and then come to Manchester for New Year."

"Yeah. Well, Nova's family used to live next door to them. And when I visited, Nova and I used to play together."

Nan's eyes widened. "Nova was the girl your parents used to call 'your little friend' when you came to see us?"

"You remember that?"

"I do because you used to blush whenever she was mentioned! Your grandad used to tease you and say she was your girlfriend!"

I rolled my eyes, although a strange feeling passed through me at her words. I remembered the teasing. Of course, I was nine when I first met Nova, and I had no interest in girls. She was my friend. The fact she had grown up to be beautiful was rather irrelevant since I wasn't hanging around beyond Christmas.

"Anyway," I went on, "back then, we used to put letters through each other's doors. I don't know what they were about now, just that we did it every day I was visiting. Apparently, she thinks I need to find my Christmas spirit."

An uncharacteristic snort shot from Nan, and she covered her mouth, even though it was too late to conceal it. "The girl's got a point, Donovan."

She probably did. But did I *want* to enjoy a small-town Christmas? I'd already re-written Christmas by not being traditional for most of the past ten years, yet she thought I needed to go back to my roots.

"She wants to do some things we did as kids, I think," I said, glancing down at the note again. Her cryptic clues didn't give me much to go with, aside from that 'Slip not' probably meant ice skating. We had done that before. Well, I did. Nova clung to the side of the rink like it was going to disappear and her dad had pushed her around the ice, even though she was terrified.

Why can I remember so much of this now?

"Well, I think she's right," Nan said, placing her hand over mine. "You should re-connect with her. It certainly couldn't do you any harm."

I stared at my grandmother, really looking at her for the first time since I'd arrived. When I was younger, I only got to visit her once a year. Twice at the most because of school and distance, and then once we moved to Italy, she and Grandad came to see us a few times. Back then, Nan had blonde but greying hair. She used to wear it so it fell straight, just below her shoulders. My grandad was also quite short—I got my height from the other side of my family. Grandad Trevor had a full head of brown hair peppered with white streaks. He also had the best sense of humour. Used to drive Nan crazy because he rarely took anything seriously. Not that Nan was overly serious, she just had more concern for things. Probably something that stemmed from her being the one to run the household while he worked. Everything fell on her, from cooking and cleaning to parenting duties. She loved to do it, but it meant a lot of responsibility fell on her, at least until my mum had left home.

But I didn't know them. Not their likes and dislikes. Favourite foods, favourite TV shows. I didn't know how it must have felt when their family moved away. How it felt to miss their child and grandchild. And in my rush to do my own growing up and exploring of the world, I'd just kind of... forgotten about them. Not completely, obviously. But while I checked in with my parents regularly, they were the only ones I spoke to often. I saw the rest of my family's updates on social media, messaged them now and again. But Nan and Grandad didn't use social media. They emailed, but I often forgot to get back to them. I called them so rarely, swept up in my own adventures.

Now, Nan sat peering at me through her rectangular glasses, looking smaller than ever. Her personality and will were as strong as they always had been, but what Nova said earlier continued to run through my mind. Although my nan's questioning at the market wasn't handled well, I was almost a stranger to her now. Neither of us knew each other anymore. I couldn't change my feelings about wanting to be travelling again; I'd been doing it for so long it was fully engrained in me to keep on moving. But Nova was right. Nan's lifelong companion was gone. I couldn't begin to imagine how that felt. Since I'd arrived, I'd done nothing but sleep and clash with her. Sure, I was tired and jetlagged, but that wasn't her fault.

"Are you all right, Donovan?" she asked, and I blinked to pull myself out of my thoughts. I wasn't ready to face that conversation with her just yet.

"Yeah. I was just thinking about what you said about Nova. I guess I don't have much else planned while I'm here, other than doing some things with you."

I was sure surprise crossed her face for a moment, but she smiled. "Well, Nova still has to work, so there's time for us during the week."

"What do you do during the week?" I asked. "Are there places you go to? People you meet?"

That flash of surprise again. "I always go to The Smugglers on Tuesdays to meet my friends for lunch. I meet Maureen for coffee every Thursday morning in town, and most days I go somewhere for a walk just to get out of the house for a while."

I nodded thoughtfully. I remembered going to The Smugglers Inn once or twice. From my recollection, they did a daily carvery that was always delicious. Amazing views over the fields and the sea too. I made a note to go in for a drink. It wasn't too far from Nan's house; easily walkable for me.

"Is there anywhere you'd like to go while I'm here?" I asked. "Because I have the hire car, so we can go anywhere you want to."

Her eyes softened, and she smiled. "I'll have a think and we can choose some things to do together."

"Okay," I said, smiling back at her. I picked up Nova's note. "Do you have a pen and some paper, please? And an envelope? I think I'm going to answer Nova's letter."

Nan stood up and walked over to the wide drawer in the TV unit. She bent down and opened it, then straightened and handed me the things I had asked for. "There you go," she said. "Now, go and accept her invitation."

I laughed, a little lighter just for having a better conversation with my nan. As she sat back down on the sofa, I shuffled off and sat on the floor so I could rest on the coffee table.

I hadn't written anyone a letter in years, and a weird bubble of nostalgia washed over me. Something I hadn't felt in a while because I rarely looked back unless I'd had a few too many drinks. I was always looking forward to the next big adventure, but maybe that was what *this* was. On a much smaller scale, but also, maybe it was what I could use for my blog for the next few weeks. I usually scheduled stuff in advance about where I had been, letting people believe I was on a city break somewhere, while in reality, I was sunbathing by a swimming pool. This would be an interesting change of pace for me.

Holding the pen to the paper, I thought about what I wanted to say. First, I picked up Nova's letter from the couch and re-read it. Although I could tell from her tone she was a bit pissed off with me about my blog post—which, to me, was not a slating of the town but more my personal thoughts; something else I rarely let people see—there was something sweet about this idea. I was confident I would never be excited about Christmas the way I once had been. There was something endearing about her, though. Even if we butted heads a lot, it would be good to be around someone other than my grandmother.

> *Nova,*
> *The Christmas hit list sounds like a killing spree. I know you said you like true crime documentaries, but I don't want to be the subject of one.*
>
> *However, I am willing to accept your challenge, but I'm warning you in advance... the cynicism is strong. If you can locate the Christmas spirit in my cold, grumpy—yes, I remember you calling me that—heart, I will apologise and rock up at your house on Christmas morning dressed as an elf.*

I wished I could insert emojis with a pen and paper. I changed the full stop to an exclamation mark, hoping it conveyed that I was mostly kidding. I truly didn't think there would be a part of me that would enjoy a small-town Christmas again. It was too fucking cold and grey.

> *I pick Slip not first because I think it's ice skating, and I want to see if you have improved since the last time we went. Just let me know when you want to go, and I'll be there!*

I chuckled to myself as I put the note in the envelope, ready to post through Nova's letterbox. Standing, I let Nan know I was going to deliver it, and then tugged on my shoes to take it next door.

I'd only been back in the house for fifteen minutes before her response dropped onto the doormat. Nan grinned as I got up to collect it, and I thought about how, when we were kids, we were only allowed to go out until it got dark. As adults, this shit could have gone on all night, so I decided I'd respond to whatever she said in the morning. I pulled at the envelope's flap to open it and yanked out the new note.

> Get your elf costume ready.
> Ice skating at Exeter's Winter Wonderland on Saturday.
> I will confirm the time ASAP. Happy to drive us or go in your car.
> As for the killing spree, my money is on me throttling you before the end of the Christmas holidays.

I laughed out loud, then continued reading the last line.

> I know we're only next door, but it's freezing outside and I want to put my PJs on, so here's my number. Text with any further thoughts you have.

It was like she'd read my mind. I looked at her number, then took out my phone to program it in. Once I'd saved it, I typed:

> Saturday is good. P.S You won't throttle me. My sarcastic charm will keep me safe. :D

Two minutes later, she text back:

> We'll see.

CHAPTER 7

NOVA

MY WORK WEEK FLEW BY IN A FLURRY OF CHRISTMAS MUSIC AND CRAFT projects, mingled with lessons I'd managed to put a seasonal spin on. When I'd popped in to see June on Friday afternoon, Donovan had gone out. I wondered if that was deliberate since he now knew I always came over on Friday afternoons. June had assured me that wasn't the case, though. He'd gone out to Trago Mills and hadn't returned yet. It didn't surprise me. The place was a labyrinth of bargains, and I'd spent many hours in there browsing the shelves and wandering around the grounds, looking for the peacocks that roamed freely. June told me that, through the week, Donovan had taken her shopping in Exeter, and they'd also gone for lunch at the House of Marbles. I didn't pry into whether their relationship was improving, but she didn't complain about him, so I guessed things were better.

Donovan and I had exchanged a couple of texts during the week to confirm our ice skating plans. I wished I was better at cryptic clues as I hadn't wanted him to guess anything I had planned, but I was too eager to get things in motion to think of anything super clever.

I was amused by the comments he'd made in his note to me about dressing in an elf costume and his teasing about my bad ice skating as a youngster. I wasn't entirely sure whether he was being a dick or not, but I guessed time would tell.

Surprisingly, our journey to Northernhay Gardens went well. Donovan told me about what he and June had done over the past few days. Even though she had told me some of it herself, I enjoyed hearing it from his side. He was still fairly detached when he spoke about her, but I liked that he was making an effort.

Once inside Exeter's version of Winter Wonderland, skates on and at the edge of the rink, I wavered. The rink was busy, with lots of parents and children skating around. I wasn't exactly an expert on the ice, but I had grown more competent since I was a child. However, I hadn't skated for around five years, so I wasn't sure how I would fare. I'd also forgotten how cold ice rinks were. Yes, there is a clue in the name, but somehow, in my head, it seemed like it should be warmer than it truly was.

"Nervous?" Donovan asked with a smirk as we stood near the entrance to the rink. He was wearing a thick beige V-neck jumper and blue jeans, his denim jacket over the top, and his blue scarf around his neck. Tall and stocky as he was, I wondered if he would be steady or shaky on his skates.

"Apprehensive," I corrected. "I haven't done this in a while." I tucked my hands inside my black coat for a moment, trying to suppress a shiver.

"Me neither, so I guess we're pretty even."

I nodded, taking a deep breath. I hadn't thought about how this would work. I had no intention of holding his hand—we weren't a couple on a date. But if we just went off on our own, we weren't really skating together.

"Come on," Donovan said, stepping around me and setting his blades on the ice. "Let's just go around slowly."

"I don't think you're supposed to go slowly," I replied, taking tentative steps onto the ice behind him. "That's how you fall over."

He moved forward a couple of paces so we were both properly on the inside edge of the rink. There were tiny children speeding around as if they'd been born with skates attached to their feet, and adults at varying levels of competence. Some wobbly, some cautious, some laughing as they whizzed around.

Come on, Nova. This is supposed to be a way to remind Donovan about having festive fun. You can't stay here the whole time.

Before I could move forward, Donovan reached for my hand. It was warm and enveloped mine easily. His touch totally shocked me because... well, he hadn't touched me before, and I'd *just* decided that hand-holding was not going to happen. I looked up at him, and he laughed.

"I can let go if you want," he said, but he'd already started skating, and I had no choice but to move too unless I wanted to fall over.

"No, it's fine," I answered, trying not to sound as weirded out as I felt. Not that his hand in mine was bad. In fact, it was strangely comforting when I was uneasy about my skills. But I was extremely conscious that my heart had started to beat faster, and I hoped it was only because of my nerves about skating.

"I'm guessing when you suggested this, you meant for us to do more than one lap and then go home?"

I snorted, finding my rhythm and pushing thoughts of my racing heart aside. "I didn't come all this way and pay for just the one go around. We have forty-five minutes, but we don't have to stay for all of it."

"Do you have plans after this, or are we just going our separate ways?"

The tone of teasing in his voice was one I was being forced to quickly get used to. I couldn't decide if he was getting a kick out of my little plan in the way I hoped he would or if he was just humouring me.

"Good question," I said. "I mean, there are plenty of options. We could check out the rest of Winter Wonderland, go to the Exeter Christmas market, or we could do something else from the list."

"Let's see how we get on with the skating first. If you aren't ready to strangle me by the end of it, we can decide then."

I risked a look up at him, and his lips were twitching as if he was trying to stop a smile.

He was mocking me.

"It was brave of you to wear a scarf," I said. "That would be the perfect murder weapon."

"All this talk of murder is making me paranoid."

"You were the one who brought it up," I pointed out.

"True. So, how does this work, then? We have the list, and we have very limited time to fit everything in."

"That's why I kept it short. But..." I paused. "Are you still planning to leave immediately after Christmas? Because I'll be off work until the beginning of January."

"I haven't booked a flight yet," he admitted. "I think I'll go to Italy once my parents are back from their cruise, but that won't be until the tenth of January."

"I'm surprised you've considered staying that long." I meant to sound like I was joking, but I was still a little miffed by his blog post. He *hadn't* said anything bad about Dawlish, but it was odd to me that he viewed life here as something to change. That the locals, or more specifically me, should want something more.

"Nova, come on," he said. "You need to lighten up a little. Don't take what I wrote so personally."

"It was less the writing and more the way you give me that *look*," I told him, unable to keep the distaste from my voice this time.

"What look?" he asked, weaving us through the other skaters with ease.

"Judgy. Like because I don't want to fly away somewhere exotic that I'm somehow not interesting."

"It's not..."

His last words were halted as he lost concentration for a second, slipping, and his ankle seemed to bend at a horrible angle as he let go of my hand before falling to the floor and skidding across it a little.

"Shit," I hissed, skating across to him where he was doubled over, holding onto his ankle. Other people had, of course, seen him go down. While many had swerved to avoid him, unable to slow down in time, a few people stopped to come to our aid.

One of the stewards had also seen us, and he pushed his way

through to attend to Donovan while I watched on, stunned at how fast it had all happened. One minute, we were engaging in our usual frenemy kind of way, and the next, Donovan had hit the ground.

"Are you okay, sir?" the steward asked. Some of the crowd moved away, satisfied the injured stranger had got help, while others just moved back but continued to watch.

"Nope," Donovan said, his voice pained. "Not okay at all."

"Do you think you can stand up?"

"Not sure. I may be able to with help."

I moved back a little further as a man who had been watching everything came forward to offer his assistance. They both supported Donovan, heaving him up to his feet, but as he tried to put weight on his injured leg, he cried out.

"Okay," the steward said. "Take it easy. We need to get you off the ice. We're going to ease you out of here, and then we can get your boot off. Just keep as much of your weight as you can on your good foot."

Donovan nodded, but I couldn't see his expression as I was behind him now. Thankfully, we weren't far from the edge, and the guys took all his weight and helped him off the ice, with me following.

I hoped he hadn't broken his ankle; that was going to do nothing for his opinions about Christmas or my activities. A stab of guilt pierced through me. Maybe this was a stupid idea. Ice skating was dangerous, and even though it wasn't exactly guaranteed that someone would get hurt, it was always a possibility. Now, I might have knackered his ankle and his Christmas.

Once Donovan was off the ice, he hobbled over to the nearest bench, and the two men helped him to sit down. Pain was clearly written across Donovan's face, and that ripple of guilt washed through me again. As the steward used his radio to call the medics in, I sat down on the bench beside Donovan. I didn't know what to say to him, so I just sat quietly, praying I hadn't permanently damaged him.

"The medics are coming," the steward said, and the man who had assisted nodded and patted Donovan's shoulder.

"Hope you get sorted out quickly, mate."

"Thanks," Donovan said, returning the guy's nod with one of his own.

The first aid station was just outside the ice rink, so it took less than two minutes for a medic to come in and assess the situation. After removing Donovan's ice skates and examining his ankle, which was severely swollen, the medic said it was badly sprained, but he was confident it was not broken. Once we were given some instructions on how to take care of the injury and things to look out for that would suggest something was amiss, the medics told me I could go and get my car and bring it to one of the side streets because there was no way he'd be able to walk as far as the car park. The medics were able to provide a wheelchair to get Donovan from the rink to my car, but I didn't know how me and June would get him into the house. He had been bandaged up and given some paracetamol for the pain, and I'd had to push my car's passenger seat as far back as it would go to allow him as much space as possible.

Once we were on the road, anxiety churned in my stomach.

"Donovan, I'm so sorry," I said, glancing at him for a second. His head was resting back against the headrest, his eyes closed.

"What for?" he asked.

"I should never have suggested ice skating." *Or maybe any of this.* It was clear any friendship we'd had as children was pretty much gone now we'd had our own life experiences and grown different personalities. It had seemed fun when I'd suggested it. I'd intended to show him there was more to life than travelling. That there was still magic to be found if he was willing to look. Sure, he had agreed to it. And he'd done so with a reasonable amount of good humour. Even so, he probably never wanted to be landed with Seasonal Sally from next door.

"I knew what I was getting in to." From the corner of my eye, I saw his head turn towards me, and I wriggled awkwardly. I was sure my face was beginning to glow, knowing I was the cause of his pain, even if he was being nice about it.

"Yeah, but did you really want to come? Or did you just do it because... Why did you come?"

I risked another glimpse his way and his wrinkled forehead suggested he was confused by the question. "Nova, I'm in Devon visiting my grandma. I know nobody here aside from you, and even though the link between us isn't exactly the strongest, I wasn't sure what I was going to do while I was here. And that's not to say I don't want to spend time with Nan, but three or four weeks is long when you only know one person. So, I came with you because I thought it would be fun. And because I haven't been ice skating for years. And because, even though you continually threaten to murder me, which you almost succeeded at today..." I cringed, and he grinned, "I'm not totally closed-minded. I *don't* think there is anything left in Dawlish for me anymore, but I might as well make the most of my time here. It beats sitting around in Nan's house or driving around trying to find things to do on my own."

I raised an eyebrow. "I thought you liked being on your own."

Another eye flick his way. He hesitated before saying, "It's different here. I already know what's around for the most part. When I'm in a different country, a lot of it is about the unexpected."

"Seems dangerous. Don't you research where you're going?"

"To a degree. But I like to look around and find things off the main tourist trails. That's beside the point. You asked me to do something with you, and what do I have to lose?"

"Your ankle, apparently," I muttered, the lurking guilt hitting me again.

"What happened today was an accident. Nothing more, nothing less. It might limit any other things you have planned for me, though."

I thought over my list, surprised to find I was relieved that wasn't the case. "Actually, everything else I have planned involves sitting down. Maybe one thing might require a shopping trip, and another is better standing up, but I could find something for you to sit on."

Had I not been driving, I would have closed my eyes and hoped to disappear. I heard the words I'd just said, the double entendre screaming at me. Donovan laughed out loud as my cheeks burned.

"Not the first time a woman has said that to me," he said, and I squirmed in discomfort.

"I didn't mean that how it sounded," I said, wishing my car came with an ejector seat to propel me away from this situation. I remembered my fleeting thought that, had I met him in any other way than I did, his attractiveness would have got my attention.

I couldn't afford to look at him again, my focus staying firmly on the road ahead, trying to shift that idea from my mind.

"Sure, sure," he teased, still laughing.

"Oh my God, please stop." But then a laugh bubbled out of my lips too. It was all I could do. It had been so long since I'd been around a man who wasn't a colleague that I'd forgotten what it felt like to have an accidental slip of the tongue that caused blushing and laughter.

"Okay, we'll move on." He chuckled once more. "Really, though. Don't worry about today. Hopefully, a few days of resting will sort it out."

"Not sure June will thank me for bringing you home in this state." I nodded towards his foot.

"She'll love it. She'll get to fuss over me and spoil me."

"Ha! She might make you a cup of tea, but she'll probably tell you to shake it off!"

I was kidding, mostly. June used to be a nurse, so there was nobody better to keep an eye on him. However, she was the more no-nonsense kind. So, while she would ensure his ankle was healing as it should, she wouldn't be a slave to him either.

"Come inside with me. Lay it on thick. I'm in agony here!" Donovan said, with mock indignation.

All I could do was snigger, but when he winced, I said, "I'm sorry. I know it hurts. Sprained ankles are horrible. I once sprained mine after a few too many glasses of wine due to a pair of demon high heels."

"I can't imagine you drunk."

"Nor do you want to," I said. "It's not pretty."

"Which kind are you?"

"What do you mean?"

"Which kind of drunk? You know, loud, sad, funny? People usually fall into one of those categories."

"Ah, yes. I become honest. Like... disturbingly honest."

"Noted. In that case, no alcohol around me. I can't help thinking you're honest enough with me."

The now-familiar lip twitch caught my attention, and even though he was messing with me, I'd perhaps been a little harder on him than I would have been on anyone else I knew so little about. We'd gotten off to such a rubbish start, though, with him instantly bristling at the sight of me as if I was some scammer trying to get my hands on his grandmother's prized possessions. Maybe, on realising he was someone I used to know, I'd been less lenient on him instead of more, hoping he would fit back into my memory of who he used to be. I hadn't expected him to be a gigantic child, I just hoped *something* I remembered about him would still be true. But that wasn't really fair. While I'd been through pretty standard growing-up situations, I hadn't experienced anything that turned my world upside down. He had continuously been moved from place to place, leaving behind friends, making new ones, then leaving them behind too. He'd seen things. Maybe some that had tainted his world view, and I didn't know anything about any of it.

"I may have been a little harsh," I admitted. "I'm sorry."

He shook his head. "No need. I haven't exactly been an angel since I got here."

"True." I grinned to let him know I wasn't upset about it. "Maybe we should just start again... again."

"Okay. But if we fall out this time, no more second chances."

He was also smiling, and I laughed. "Deal."

When we got back home, I parked outside June's house, then got out of my car and went to the passenger side to open the door and help Donovan out. I wasn't sure how I would deliver him from the car to the house, but after a bit of a struggle to get him to his feet, we carefully hobbled down the path. Donovan only had one shoe on, and he was leaning on me heavily for support, hissing in sharp breaths every time he had to put weight on his sprained ankle. It was no easy feat since he was a foot taller than me and a lot heavier with his sturdy build. We had only gotten halfway down the path when the front door opened, and June's hand covered her mouth as she saw the state of her grandson.

"Oh my God," she said, stepping down onto the path and meeting us where we'd paused for a break. She glanced at Donovan before circling around to his other side.

"It's okay, Nan," he said as she wrapped an arm around his back. "It's just a sprain."

"Well, we need to put ice on that immediately. Let's get you inside."

Although June couldn't take much of Donovan's weight, having her on his other side made it a little easier for us to get to the house a bit quicker. We managed to lean him against the wall in the hallway while he took off his coat, then we helped him to the sofa in the living room, where he flopped down in relief, tugging off his scarf.

"Thank you," he said, laying the scarf over the arm of the sofa, then wiping his brow. Despite the cold, that amount of struggle combined with the pain had led to a layer of sweat forming on his forehead.

"No worries," I said, as June lifted his injured ankle onto the coffee table to keep it elevated.

"Give me your other foot," June said, bending down. "Let's get your shoe off, and then I'll go and get you some ice."

"Shall I put the kettle on?" I asked as she wrestled his trainer off while he rested his head on the back of the sofa with his eyes closed.

"Please," June replied.

"Teas all round?"

"Yes, please," Donovan answered.

"I'll also run out to the car and get your other shoe," I said, already heading to the kitchen.

Within ten minutes, everyone was settled in June's comfy living room. Donovan held a mug of tea, his injured leg now propped up more on the coffee table with a couple of cushions underneath it and a bag of frozen peas wrapped in a tea towel resting over the top. In spite of his protests, June had put a thick grey blanket over him, and he honestly looked exhausted. The pain and drama of our morning were finally getting to him, and he looked like he needed a nap.

"So, your first mission didn't get off to a great start," June said with a slight giggle. I knew she wasn't amused at Donovan's injury, more the fact that we had got home from ice skating within an hour and a half when we should have been out way longer.

"You can laugh," Donovan said, "but now I'm broken, I won't be able to drive us anywhere until I'm healed again. I can't walk very far either."

He actually sounded disappointed about it, which was a vast improvement from before. Perhaps his time with June had made him realise family was a good thing, not something to be irritated by.

June gave a sincere smile. "That doesn't matter, love. You're still here, which is what's important. It's a shame we won't be able to go to Darts Farm tomorrow, though."

Darts Farm was one of my favourite places to go to at Christmas. The farm shop in Topsham was full of everything anyone could ever need, and they sold the most exceptional locally sourced foods and drinks, as well as many other amazing things. I had bought hampers as Christmas gifts from there in the past, and their restaurant was so popular there was always a queue to get in.

"If you want a ride, I can take you," I said. "I don't have anything planned for tomorrow. If you want to go, I can drop you off and go visit my mum and dad until you're ready to leave."

"That's so kind, my darling, but I can't expect you to do that," June said. "Thank you for the offer, though."

"Would it involve a lot of walking?" Donovan asked, his eyes closed again. "Because I'm not sure I could manage too much."

It occurred to me that he had probably never been there, but with his love of local cream and Christmassy foods, I knew he would enjoy it. However, the place was pretty big and perhaps a bit much for someone with a bad sprain.

But then I remembered something. "Oh! My dad has a spare pair of crutches at his place. He still plays football and is prone to hurting his knee. I'm sure you could borrow them for a few days to help you get around."

Donovan's eyes opened, and he stared at me for a moment, something like questions in his eyes. What I'd offered seemed pretty basic to me. He had a problem, and I had a potential solution, yet his gaze seemed to search mine as if wondering why I would offer to help.

"If he doesn't mind and you're okay to take us, I would like to go. But... you don't have to stay at your parents' place. You can come with us if you want to."

From across the room, I spotted a small smile gracing June's lips, but I pretended not to see.

"I can give my dad a call and see what he says. But he won't mind at all."

CHAPTER 8

DONOVAN

ON SUNDAY MORNING, THE SWELLING ON MY ANKLE HAD GONE DOWN A little, but it still hurt like a bitch to put weight on it. Nova had confirmed her dad said I could borrow his crutches, and we swung around to their place before heading to Darts Farm with Nan. Her mum had been the one to come to the door, and she waved at me enthusiastically while I waited in the car. When I waved back, she grinned, leaning in to whisper something to Nova. I could see Nova's shoulders stiffen even in her thick coat, but when she turned around to walk back to the car, she was laughing, a faint glow on her cheeks, probably from the chill in the air.

HAVING CRUTCHES MADE GETTING AROUND MUCH EASIER, EVEN THOUGH pressing on them for so long hurt my hands. It was worth it to look around the enormous farm shop. We'd picked up some freshly made chicken and ham pies for lunch, and I'd treated everyone to a slice of cheesecake each. Nova and Nan both bought some gifts, and Nova also got some bottles of Sicilian lemonade that was made locally, which intrigued me.

· · ·

WE'D SPENT WELL OVER AN HOUR LOOKING AROUND, AND EVEN I COULD admit the winter vibe and the Christmas music were easy to be swept up in, especially when Nan and Nova were having such a good time. They were both excitedly pointing out things they liked the look of and laughing with glee as they discussed what they were going to buy. It was adorable. Something I hadn't experienced since I was with my ex, Paige. She loved to shop with her friends, and her happiness had always made me smile. This was different somehow, though. I couldn't pinpoint why, but even my cynical heart enjoyed the trip, whereas with Paige, I liked her being happy, but I only tolerated the shopping.

Once we got back to Nan's house, she heated up the pies, and we ate lunch, including the slices of cheesecake and a bottle each of Nova's Sicilian lemonade, which was really tasty.

When we were done, Nan wanted to go and watch TV, and against my better judgement, I selected 'Festive flashbacks' from Nova's hit list. I waited at Nan's kitchen table while Nova went back to her place to get the things we would need.

She returned with a small tote bag and placed it on the table in front of me before taking off her black knee-high boots. I tried hard not to look at her toned legs as she did so, but it was difficult not to appreciate them in her tight jeans.

"Okay," she said. "Since you need to keep resting, this was the best thing you could have picked." She nodded towards the bag for me to look inside, and I reached for it and pulled it towards me.

I peered into the top and laughed when I saw the edges of some DVD cases. Pulling them out, I said, "A movie afternoon, huh? That sounds good." Unsure what she'd picked, I took a look through. In front of me were *Home Alone, The Nightmare Before Christmas, Miracle on 34th Street,* and *Hook.* "Oh, wow. I don't think I've watched a Christmas movie since I was a teenager."

Nova smiled. "We won't have time to watch them all today, but we can manage one or two before one of you throws me out. Also, I know *Hook* isn't technically a Christmas movie, but we did watch it at Christmas, so it counts."

"I remember." We'd also pretended to be pirates afterwards and had pretend swordfights in my grandad's kitchen. After a pause, I added, "Although... Nan has taken over the TV in the living room, so..." Disappointment crossed her face. "There's a DVD player and a TV in my room, though." My face twisted into a questioning kind of grimace. Asking a girl who usually disliked me to my room was weird, but she was the one who'd come at me with old-fashioned technology. With Netflix and Disney Plus, people watched DVDs less. It occurred to me we could watch at least some of the movies on the subscription streaming apps on my iPad, but we'd still need somewhere comfortable to sit.

Her eyes widened for a second, and again, that blush crept up her cheeks. I wasn't sure she knew the setup of my nan's spare room, but there was a double bed in there, and very little space for much else aside from the chest of drawers the TV and DVD player stood on. On the plus side, the screen was at least reasonably sized. However, the lack of space meant the only place to sit was the bed.

"We could just go over to my house," she suggested, her questioning grimace matching mine.

I wondered what was causing the red tint to her cheeks. There was not a single hint that she was into me, so I was pretty sure it wasn't that. She'd had at least one boyfriend before because she'd mentioned him when we were talking about travelling, so she definitely wasn't new to being alone with a man. Maybe it was simply about the potential awkwardness of being on a bed with a virtual stranger.

"But we're already here," I pointed out. "And it's easier for me to get upstairs than put my shoe on and go around to yours."

Nova shrugged. "I suppose that's true." With a nod, she said, "Okay, upstairs it is."

As I used my crutches to help me get to my feet, Nova put the small pile of DVDs back into the bag and picked it up, and I poked my head around the door to tell my nan what we were doing. It felt fucking ridiculous, like I was a teenager asking for permission to take my girlfriend to my room. I half expected her to tell me to leave the door open, but instead, she just raised an eyebrow and nodded.

56

It took me a bit longer than usual to get up the stairs, but once we were there, I pointed to the door that led to my room, and Nova opened it and stepped inside. For an older person's house, the room was pretty modern. The walls were a deep blue, and the wall behind the bed had matching dark blue wallpaper with large black and white feathers all over it. Thick blue curtains hung over the windows, and the quilt cover was white with dark blue feathers on.

"This is cute," Nova said, looking around. "I've never been in here before."

"Just as well I don't have much stuff, though," I said. "Not much storage space."

She laughed. "Yeah. My spare room is an office, though there is a sofa bed that will just about fit in around my desk."

Having just watched her take off those boots, an inappropriate thought about her on a desk crossed my mind, and I pushed it away as fast as it had arrived.

I shouldn't be thinking about her that way.

"You okay?" she asked.

"Yeah." I shook my head. "Sorry. I was just thinking about... snacks."

A wide smile crossed her face as she held up the bag. "I have snacks in here."

"You thought of everything."

"I tried to. Why don't you get settled and I'll get the movie set up. What do you want to watch first?"

"You choose," I said, sitting down on the bed and leaning my crutches against the bedside table.

She nodded, and I shuffled across the bed while she pulled out *The Nightmare Before Christmas*. She'd picked the shortest movie by far, and I wondered if that was so she didn't have to stay in my room for too long. Maybe we *should* have gone to her place. I wasn't totally lying when I said going there would have been more challenging, but a bigger part of me wanted to see how she was around me when it was just the two of us and a movie. Neither of us talking or focusing on going somewhere.

In less than a minute, the movie menu screen was on the TV, and she sat down on the bed, placing the remote between us and then grabbing the bag of DVDs and snacks towards her. She put that between us too, creating a decent barrier, although I wasn't sure if it was deliberate. She'd shown no signs that she was fighting to keep her hands off me, and she wasn't uncomfortable around me either.

Maybe you're reading too much into this.

I probably was. Spending so much time alone allowed me to watch people. Analyse them. But Nova didn't need analysing. She didn't have any weird ulterior motive for being around me. She'd made what she wanted perfectly clear in the note she'd written. And while I still didn't believe she had a hope in hell of getting me to believe in Christmas magic again, being around her was definitely making this trip in the UK more bearable.

Nova pulled out a gigantic bag of popcorn followed by a bar of Galaxy and a bar of Dairy Milk. A flash of another memory flickered in my mind. Of a young Nova and me sitting on my grandad's sofa next to each other, giggling with glee because her mum had popped in with a bar of chocolate each for us. Galaxy was Nova's favourite and Dairy Milk was mine. We'd sat there watching Christmas films, breaking off pieces of chocolate and working up to a massive sugar high. We'd had several afternoons like that. Sometimes with popcorn and sometimes with chocolate.

"In my defence," Nova began, "I bought all these snacks not knowing we would have eaten a massive lunch before you picked the movie thing. So, if you're full, you can eat the chocolate later. I'm diving into the popcorn, though."

Shaking my head, I said, "How did you remember all this?"

"Honestly, I'd forgotten most of it until I had this idea to help you appreciate life back here and remember what Christmases used to be like." She shrugged. "I know I probably seem like some Christmas-obsessed weirdo, but I'm not. And I'm also fully aware we're grown adults and this is all kinds of silly. But you're so serious a lot of the time. I don't pretend to know why, or if there are reasons for that, but I do know it's not good for you to always be so focused on getting to the next place. To not stop and see what is right in front of you. I'm not trying to recreate our childhood. I just wanted to show you that letting loose and doing something mindless is okay."

She looked a little uncomfortable, like she believed I'd been judging her and thinking she was a nutcase who only wanted to do seasonal activities and nothing else mattered.

"Nova," I said, taking the chocolate bars from her and putting them on the bed. "I know what you're trying to do. I get it. I wasn't thinking anything bad about any of this. I guess I just don't fully understand why it matters to you."

"I hadn't got that far in figuring it out," she said with a small laugh. "Mostly, I think it's that I know how close your family used to be, and... I've seen what your nan has been through. She misses your parents. She misses having her daughter here, and I know the two of you have had your moments, but she likes you being around." She paused and sighed. "Sorry. This wasn't meant to be a guilt trip. I'm just saying... family is important."

I nodded. "Yeah. It is." A wave of well-suppressed grief hit me, and I swallowed the lump in my throat. "You know, I left home when I was young. Thought I had all the time in the world. I wanted to see as many places as I could, so I skipped out on university to do it. I've been to Australia, Thailand, Mexico, the USA, Canada, Hawaii, Jamaica, Japan, various places in Europe, the Philippines, and New Zealand. And I had the best time, not worrying about anything much. But then... my grandad died." I paused, wondering why the hell I was dumping all this on her and where it had come from. I guessed months of pretending nothing bothered me had finally reached the surface when faced with so many reminders of what I'd missed out on. "I *wanted* to come home for his funeral, but I just... I was too scared to. I was afraid my parents and Nan would all be judging me for not coming over to visit more. For not calling them more. It seemed almost hypocritical to be at his funeral when I barely saw him when he was alive. I don't have a big family, so when I went away, I didn't think I would miss much. It's not like I have brothers and sisters who'd be getting married and having kids. Mum and Dad certainly weren't having any more children, and anyone else was too distant to be a concern. Losing Grandad was like a slap in the face, though." Glancing at Nova, I checked she hadn't nodded off while I was spilling my guts, but she hadn't. She was listening intently. "I know I'm moody and hard to get to know, and I know my need to get out of here makes me seem like I don't give a shit, but I do. I just don't know how to process everything that's happened. How to explain all the things that feel different now I've been away for so long."

A strange, unfamiliar ache began in my chest, and I drew in a slow breath, trying to ease it away. This was exactly why I didn't talk about all those things. I'd only scratched over the surface and it had triggered something inside me. I wasn't the kind of person who bottled everything up until it exploded. I'd talked about losing my grandad while I was away, but connecting with my family was harder somehow.

"There's no time limit on it," Nova said softly. "And if you want to be close to your nan again, then be close to her. When you go away, stay in touch. Reach out. Answer when she reaches out to you. It's not so hard, you know?"

I smiled. "It's really hard to disagree with you when you speak common sense."

"It's what I do."

It did seem to be. She had this strange way of seeing through me. I wasn't sure if I was okay with it or not, but I also didn't seem to have a choice. There were things about me she couldn't know unless I told her, but she *had* seen something in me I tried to hide. The fact that I did care about things. And it wasn't so much that I *tried* to hide it, more that it had got buried. Being on my own for so long had made me selfish in some ways. I still had a normal level of human decency, politeness, and manners where other people were concerned. I am British, after all. But I'd got so caught up in what I was doing, and the people I'd left in the UK had been disconnected. I hadn't meant for it to happen, but it did, and Grandad's sudden death only showed me that more clearly.

I knew for sure that if Nova hadn't known me as a kid, she

wouldn't have ever entertained the idea of being with me now, not after the way I'd acted when I first saw her. She was looking for the parts of me she liked before now she knew who I was. Even as a child, she had been a nurturer. The kind of person who looks out for others, shows kindness, and looks for the best in everyone, whereas I was always looking for the twist. The hidden agenda.

Just like I'd done when I first re-met her.

"Nova, I know I already apologised, but I really am sorry for the way I acted the day we met," I said. "I think..." I paused, wishing there wasn't something about her that made me want to open up. But I'd started the sentence already. Whether I wanted to admit it or not, there was still some kind of connection between us. One that was very slowly strengthening as I allowed her to take me on this weird little Christmas-themed mystery tour.

"What is it?" she asked, her brown eyes focused on mine.

This was the closest I had felt to her, or to anyone, in so long that I wasn't sure what to do with it, but I took a deep breath. "I had a girlfriend, Paige, a few years back. I met her in Australia and we travelled together for three years. From the end of our first year together, she talked about us settling down. She wanted us to get married and live in Australia, where she was from. I loved her, but I wanted to keep moving. We went to so many places together and had the best time, but eventually, she just wanted to go back to her home. When I wouldn't go, she made me feel like the worst person. Accused me of using her as a travelling sex toy, which was a fucking joke. I was crazy about her, and if I'd just wanted someone to sleep with, I could have picked up anyone. I wanted her. She knew more about me than anyone ever had, and she threw it all at me when we broke up. Said I was weak and scared for not wanting to settle down. Told me my parents were trash for making me afraid to commit because we'd moved around so much when I was younger."

I paused as the memories lashed down on me. It didn't hurt anymore, but it made me angry. It had made me stubborn. The way she had gone at me had made me believe my decisions and what I wanted weren't important. They weren't even when we were together as most of the places we went to were ones she chose. That realisation had seeped into every corner of my life. Her words had triggered a defiance to do what I wanted, when I wanted, and on my terms. That's not to say it was her fault entirely. But if she hadn't responded the way she had, maybe I would have come home sooner. Maybe I would have found someone else to travel with. Maybe I wouldn't have believed I needed to be mostly on my own.

As I looked back up at Nova, her face was filled with confusion, and I wasn't surprised because she couldn't hear my thoughts and I hadn't explained how what I'd said linked to the conversation we were having.

"After Paige, there was someone else I was interested in. In fact, for a while, there were lots of people I met and wanted to hang out with. I don't just mean to date, I mean people I got to know as friends. As my blog took off, I found that many of them wanted me to shout them out in videos and stuff, just to boost their own accounts. The girl I liked was a little different. She didn't seem to be interested in me at all, then one day, she let me take her out to dinner. Before I knew it, she wanted the best of everything. Wanted me to take her to the best restaurants, buy her new clothes and shoes. Seemed a bit suspicious since she had brushed me off so many times. One night, after we'd been out drinking, we were in a hotel room and she was on her phone. She'd had so much to drink that she ran to the bathroom to throw up and left the phone open on the bed. I reached over to grab her a bottle of water from the nightstand and the screen was open to a message with a friend, laughing about how much she had got from me and saying she could get so much more once I let my guard down."

"What did you do after you saw the messages?"

"I left. Grabbed my stuff and walked out while she was throwing up in the bathroom. Because I'm not a total asshole, I still paid for her room for the night, but I didn't care about where she went after that or how she got there. I blocked her from reaching out to me, but I heard on the grapevine that she was fine and had found her way to Portugal. Probably on the back of some other mug."

Nova nodded slowly, like she was processing everything I'd told her, and her eyes were the softest I'd ever seen them while looking at me. "I'm sorry. About everything. I guess all of those things..." she trailed off. "I get it. I get why you look for the worst in people. But you've just been unlucky. Not everyone you meet is going to be a dick."

Hearing her say 'dick' made me laugh. She didn't seem the type who swore often, or maybe she was just trained that way because of being a teacher. It somehow sounded alien coming out of her mouth.

Do. Not. Make. An. Inappropriate. Comment.

As if she'd heard my thoughts, she said, "Wait until you hear me say 'fuck'."

The grin on her face and hearing the word spoken with such perfect diction did something to me. I fucking hoped my dick didn't visibly twitch, and when she blushed, still laughing, something cold within me began to thaw.

"Don't let Nan hear you say that," I teased, and she laughed again.

"Your nan swears more than I do!"

She wasn't wrong. She didn't swear in general conversation, but I had heard her cursing to herself when something wasn't going right with whatever she was doing. Sometimes it was a crossword, sometimes it was crochet, sometimes when she was cooking.

As the laughter died down, Nova said, "Shall we watch this movie, then?"

I kind of wanted to say no and keep talking to her, but we had plenty of time.

I was home for the holidays. And now, I could stay up as late as I wanted.

CHAPTER 9

NOVA

SPENDING SUNDAY WITH DONOVAN WAS... UNEXPECTEDLY INTERESTING. I'd really wanted to give him a chance to find his inner kid beneath his cold exterior. I hadn't expected him to do so quickly, and he still wasn't there yet, but he'd done something I'd expected even less. He'd opened up to me. About why he didn't trust and why he'd become so set in his ways. Some might say selfish. I couldn't pretend it wasn't true, but I kind of understood how it had happened. Being away on his own must have been a freedom like he'd never had before. Then to find someone to share it with, only for them to throw a ton of his own issues at him... it made sense that he'd dug his heels in. I wasn't saying it was smart or healthy, only that I could see how it had occurred. I would likely have run home with my tail between my legs, but as we'd established, we were very different people. Even so, we had found a bit of common ground, and we were using it to feel each other out. To find out who the other was now we were all grown up.

We watched two of the movies I'd taken over with me. *The Nightmare Before Christmas*, and *Miracle on 34th Street*. We relaxed around each other, munching the popcorn, getting gradually closer to each other on the bed. I wasn't sure how it had happened. Maybe just that every time one of us shifted position, we'd edged towards each other. We never got close enough to be touching, but the movement showed that, somehow, the gap between us as almost strangers was being bridged.

A part of me wondered... what if we hadn't moved house when I was a kid? What if Donovan's other grandad hadn't died? What if his parents hadn't moved them to Italy? Would we have continued to spend Christmases hanging out together? Would we have hit that awkward stage where boy and girl friends became complicated? Most likely, once Donovan started high school while I was still at primary, he would have decided he didn't want to hang out with a 'kid' anymore. I wondered if I would have had a crush on him, the older boy who came to stay every year. Of course, it was impossible to guess. So many things could have happened that sent us in different directions.

I liked him. Just as I had all those years ago. Except now, we were older. Arguably wiser.

And yes, he was attractive. Most especially when he flashed that lopsided smile and those little lines appeared around his eyes. They shone when he really meant it, the deep blue sparkling.

Oh, Christ.

Noting those things about him absolutely did not mean anything. It would be pointless for it to hold any importance anyway since he was leaving after Christmas. The plan had always been to show him the benefits of living in a close-knit community and experience the festive season for what it was. A time for family and fun.

ON WEDNESDAY AFTERNOON, I WALKED INTO MY HOUSE PRACTICALLY buzzing with glee. With a contented sigh, I straightened up, carrying the two bags of Christmas gifts from the children in my class into my living room. I'd had a good haul this year, with several "Best Teacher Ever" mugs, some chocolates, and a load of *Stranger Things* items.

My students know me so well.

I was looking forward to going through the gifts again over a hot chocolate, with my Christmas tree lights twinkling beside me, but first, I wanted to shower and change into something more comfy. I had plans for dinner with a couple of my friends from work, and they were coming down to Dawlish because they'd fallen in love with the carvery at The Smugglers Inn when they'd been down before. Shannen and Gaby both lived in Exeter, so they were driving down together and staying at my place for the night. I couldn't wait to celebrate the last day of term with them. There had been a staff party at the weekend, but I never really enjoyed the bigger get-togethers. I had been friends with Gaby through work for a while, but Shannen had only just started working at our school in September, so I didn't know her too well yet. From the times I'd spoken to her, she'd seemed super friendly, and Gaby had kind of taken Shannen under her wing.

After showering, I threw on some PJs while I dried my hair, then read a book until it was time for me to get ready. Since it was just a meet-up with friends, I didn't need to get overly dressed up, but it had been a while since I'd had a reason to do more than the minimal makeup. I pulled on my 'going out' jeans—they were dark blue and slightly flared at the bottom—along with a black corset-style top with short sleeves, and then sat down at my dresser, looking through my cosmetics bag. Screw it. It was the last day of term, which made this a cause for celebration. After doing my usual foundation with a touch of plum-coloured lip gloss, I added a teensy hint of bronzer, then set about creating the perfect smoky eye with champagne-coloured eyeshadow. Even though it was freezing outside, I planned to wear my black strappy heels to complete my look. They weren't too high because I intended to have a few drinks and I had no desire to spend the Christmas holiday resting my ankle with Donovan. His was a lot better now. The swelling had gone most of the way down, and he was relying on the crutches much less than he had been. I'd been over to June's for a cheeky cuppa the night before, and Donovan and I had prepared our next hit list mission, which would be taking place the following day. Now school was out, if we wanted to, we could spend more time together. The idea caused butterflies in my stomach which I continued to ignore. Since our deeper chat at the weekend, I'd told myself over and over there was nothing to think about, even though it was becoming clear that he wasn't the prick I'd first believed he was. Maybe I should have given up on the whole hit list thing just to save myself from getting any closer to him, but I couldn't pull back yet.

I scrunched at the ends of my hair, making sure the curls fell nicely around my shoulders, and when I was satisfied, I grabbed my bag, phone, purse, and keys, and headed downstairs to wait for my friends.

The Smugglers at Christmas was so freaking beautiful. A large Christmas tree stood in the small foyer by the entrance, and as I walked into the pub, the warmth hit me instantly. Not just from coming in out of the cold; the atmosphere was warm. Being mid-week, it wasn't overly busy, but there were a few people in the bar area, waiting to be served, and some others sitting at the tables down the side of the room and by the large windows that gave an impressive view over beautiful fields with the sea in the distance.

We headed inside to the bar and waited near the doors that led to the back part of the pub, where there was a pool table and more seating. As we waited, I thought my friends both looked amazing. Dressed in smart casual clothing like me, but also both made-up. Gaby's thick blonde wavy hair looked incredible, and Shannen, who had black curls, had left hers hanging loose like I had.

"What are you drinking?" Gaby asked me with a grin.

"I'd love a white wine spritzer," I said.

"Excellent choice!" Gaby placed my order, and the bartender soon came back with my wine, a vodka and Coke, and a tall glass of lemonade.

Shannen reached for the lemonade with a shrug. "I have to babysit my nephew tomorrow afternoon, so I'd rather not do that with a hangover."

"Only Shannen would be released from her job as a teacher and immediately offer herself for babysitting duties," Gaby teased as the three of us moved away from the bar and headed towards the restaurant.

"I am clearly a glutton for punishment," Shannen said. "It's a good thing he's cute."

"I love kids," I said, "but I am also very much looking forward to this break!"

It was true. I adored the children in my class. Teaching was the only thing I'd ever wanted to do, but holidays were much needed to rest and re-charge. Admittedly, I spent a lot of my days off thinking about lessons and tasks for the next term because it was such a huge part of my life, but Christmas was when I switched off the most. I wanted the time with my friends and family, and very little else mattered.

The smell of the carvery made my mouth water, and we were shown to our table to set our drinks down before going to get our food. In my opinion, there was nowhere better for a carvery, and once my turkey was carved, I piled my plate with roast potatoes, veg, stuffing and topped it with gravy.

The three of us ate until we were stuffed, occasionally getting our drinks topped up as we chatted and laughed. I was really glad the night wasn't ending anytime soon; we were having too much fun. It would have been a shame to go our separate ways.

I didn't get to do this much. Because I'd grown up mostly in Exeter and also gone to university there, the people I was closest to were either there or in further away towns or scattered across the country. Exeter wasn't far away, but still, a quick cuppa with someone took a twenty to thirty-minute drive, and during term time, my schedule didn't allow for it very often. I didn't have anyone I could just pop in to see for a chat other than June; not that that was a bad thing. I loved her, but having other friends in the immediate area was something I missed sometimes. I'd contemplated moving back to the city, but in spite of missing the company, I couldn't bring myself to go.

Once we were full and ready to go home and eat more junk food while watching movies, we headed out to the front of the pub to pay. We were in the middle of discussing which of our favourite hot guy movies to watch first when I got the strange sensation that someone was watching me. I turned around and almost immediately saw Donovan sitting alone at a table near the doors. My heart, rather annoyingly, jolted as our eyes connected.

I handed Gaby my share of money for the bill and said, "I'll be right back."

It only took a couple of strides to reach him, though I could sense the girls' eyes on me, and I said, "Hey. Wasn't expecting to see you in here."

He smiled, holding onto his beer bottle. "Nan said she comes here for lunch every week, and I thought I'd come and have a drink. I wasn't expecting to bump into you either."

I gestured over my shoulder to Gaby and Shannen, who were watching us with amused grins on their faces, which I tried to ignore. "Girls' night out to celebrate the end of term. We're having a sleepover." I grinned as I said it, like an over-excited teenager.

Donovan laughed. "Thanks for the warning. At least I'll know why there's noise coming from your place tonight."

"I don't know what you mean," I said innocently. "We're angels."

His eyes moved over to them, where they were still eyeing us with no subtlety at all. "Sure. I believe you."

As his gaze moved over Gaby, a weird prickle of something washed over me, causing a shiver to shoot through me.

"Are we still good for tomorrow?" I asked, trying to re-direct whatever that sensation was.

He nodded. "Yeah. Not sure what state you'll be in, though."

I was not even close to being drunk, and seeing him unexpectedly had somehow sobered me up a little more.

"I'll be okay," I said. "I'm not a big drinker."

Usually. Seeing him in the pub had thrown me off. He was just sitting there on his own, but what if some woman caught his attention and he...

So not my business.

I needed to get away from him because, clearly, the alcohol was having some kind of effect on me. I could do without saying anything embarrassing in front of him and my friends. Thankfully, they walked towards me, and I turned to them and said, "Are you ready to go?"

They both nodded, but I could see how badly they wanted to ask me about who this man was. Both of them gave him a once-over, and

I could tell from their grins that they approved, but Donovan had also noticed, and I was about ready to curl up into a ball of mortification.

I turned to Donovan and said, "I guess I'll see you tomorrow."

He smirked. "You will."

With a pathetic wave, I linked arms with Gaby and Shannen and we headed outside into the cold.

"Okay, spill," Gaby said while I pulled out my phone to order a taxi.

"I will when we get home, I promise. But I may need a few more drinks."

THE CAB DIDN'T TAKE LONG TO ARRIVE, AND ONCE WE WERE ALL IN OUR pyjamas and sprawled out in my living room with bowls of crisps, popcorn, and various packets of sweets on the coffee table—along with a couple of bottles of white wine—I knew I was about to get grilled.

"You have made us wait long enough!" Gaby said from her position on the sofa. She'd slung her duvet over herself and was munching on some Haribos.

I let out a small groan, heat racing across my cheeks. The thing was, it wasn't like there was much to say. Just that I didn't know what the hell I was doing anymore when it came to Donovan. "I don't know what to say," I told them honestly as I reached for my wine glass. "It's... complicated, I guess."

"So, let's talk it out," Shannen said, giving me an understanding smile. She was on my other sofa, wrapped in her duvet just like Gaby. I was going to my bed eventually, so I had a fluffy blanket slung around my shoulders where I sat on the floor, even though the house was more than warm enough.

"He's... His name's Donovan."

Gaby wolf-whistled. "That's a sexy name right there. Imagine calling that out in the throes of passion." She threw her head back in fake ecstasy, making me and Shannen laugh.

She was right. His name was sexy. *He* was sexy.

Which was something else I hadn't allowed myself to think before. His smile. His eyes. The way he smirked when he was teasing me. Even when he was being irritating, it was still hot. I put my glass back down, deciding it had loosened my tongue enough.

I gave a brief rundown of who he was, how I knew him, and what our deal was with the list, and the girls listened intently.

"The thing is," I said, "he's... I like him, but I don't think it's wise to get too close since he has no interest in staying here, and I doubt he's interested in me anyway. It's not like I want to marry him and have his babies or anything. But there's just something about him."

Shannen chuckled. "I think he's interested in you. Didn't you see the way he looked at you?"

"Like he wanted to take you home and ravage you," Gaby added, making us laugh again.

"I don't think he sees me like that," I said. "I annoy him more than anything."

"I think you're wrong." Shannen twirled her glass around in her hand. "He did a thing with his eyes when he looked at you." When I furrowed my brow, she laughed. "I don't know how to explain it. Just, when he looked at me and Gaby, he smiled and it was friendly, but when he looked at you... his eyes just looked different."

"Dilated pupils?" Gaby asked. "Lust swirling in those blue depths?"

Shannen picked up a cushion from behind her and launched it at Gaby. "You sound like a cheesy romance novel." She giggled before looking at me again more seriously. "I get why you would want to be careful. I mean, he isn't going to be here for long, so getting attached will make it hard to let him go."

"How do you feel about holiday flings?" Gaby raised an eyebrow.

"Not great," I admitted, although something inside me stirred at the idea. But I wasn't really that kind of girl. I fully supported women who wanted something quick with a guy, but it didn't feel right for me. Especially not with Donovan, and not even because he was leaving, but because of who he was. We might have been worlds apart from what we used to be, but I thought that if we were going to be *something*, it was worth more than some random quickie. Our history might not have been much, but maybe it could have been under different circumstances.

A groan fell from my lips. "I can't think about this anymore. It's not worth it."

"But you're already thinking about it," Gaby pointed out, more softly this time. "Pretending you aren't won't change how you feel."

"I don't know how I feel," I said honestly. "It's all really confusing."

"But you feel *something*."

I nodded. "Yeah, I think so."

Before anyone else could speak, my text message tone went off, and I picked up my phone with a sigh.

> **Donovan**
> You looked beautiful tonight.

My heart fluttered in my chest, my stomach flipping over at his words and possibly the shock. I leaned over and handed the phone to Shannen, and she beamed and passed it to Gaby while I processed what I'd just read.

"Okay, well that's just ruled out forgetting about it," Gaby said, grinning as she leaned over the coffee table to hand my phone back to me.

"What am I... what?" I said, staring at the screen again as if I'd somehow misread it the first time. But no. I hadn't. "Can I just say thank you?"

Shannen and Gaby both laughed, and I couldn't help joining in, allowing myself to enjoy the message for a moment.

"What do you want to say to him?" Shannen asked.

"I don't know!" I moaned, closing my eyes and resting my forehead on the coffee table. "I kinda want to see him, but I'm not going back to the pub in my pyjamas."

"Sneak into his room," Gaby teased. "Wait for him in your sexiest night clothes."

"These are my sexiest night clothes," I said, gesturing down at my candy cane-striped PJs, causing us all to start laughing again. It had been years since I owned anything other than comfy bedtime attire. I barely owned any sexy underwear anymore.

Fucking hell. Was I becoming a person who had gotten so comfortable that I didn't treat myself to nice things anymore? Had I become so settled in single life I'd given up on even trying to find someone? No, it wasn't that. I was extremely content on my own. But did that mean I shouldn't have clothing that made me feel attractive? Had I got so used to being alone that I was in a rut somehow without realising?

"Damn him," I said, lifting my head. "Him being here has got me second-guessing everything. Does not having sexy undies mean I've got boring?"

"No," Shannen said. "It means you don't see the point in buying it if you have nobody to show it to. I speak from experience."

I smiled. I knew Shannen was also single and had been for a while after breaking up with a guy everyone thought she would marry. From what I knew of her, she was from a wealthy family with high expectations, but she had decided to take her own route when it came to meeting someone. I wished I had as much confidence in myself as she had.

"You are massively overthinking this," Gaby said as she reached over for some popcorn. "You're letting his worldwide adventures taint your view of yourself. And there's nothing wrong with you. He just said you're beautiful. Just enjoy that and see what happens from here."

Wise words from my crazy friend. Gaby was a wild one, but she always came through for me when I needed her.

The fact was, Donovan and I were two very different people. People who were re-getting to know each other. An attraction might have been beginning to form, but that was all it could ever be. No point getting caught up in it, and definitely no point in getting down on myself. I loved my life as it was, and nothing was going to change that.

CHAPTER 10

DONOVAN

I LOOKED AT MY PHONE FOR ABOUT THE FIFTIETH TIME THAT MORNING, waiting for Nova to text me to tell me the next thing on our Christmas list was cancelled due to her hangover. All I could think about after I'd seen her in the pub was how gorgeous she'd looked. How different from her usual basic attire and makeup—which wasn't unappealing in any way. But out with her friends, dressed up and having fun, she was stunning.

In hindsight, telling her in a text message that she looked beautiful might not have been the best idea. I wasn't even sure how I wanted her to react. Just that, in the moment, I wanted her to know how good she looked.

She had responded with a blushing emoji and nothing else, but I figured since she hadn't told me to fuck off, everything was fine.

"Will you stop checking your phone," Nan chided as we sat in a small cafe in Dawlish's town centre. A cosy little place called Home Kitchen, just around the corner from the amusements arcade that had quite possibly been there since the dawn of time.

"Sorry," I said, sliding it off the table and back into my pocket as a tall man with dark hair set down a tray holding a teapot, two cups, and a silver jug of milk. Nan wasn't in the greatest of moods that morning, and while I'd gone out with her only to stop the boredom of being in the house on my own, I was glad I had because she was a little off for some reason.

"I'll be glad when you're out from under my feet this afternoon," she muttered as she picked up the teapot and poured some tea into her cup.

The door opened behind me, and I turned on instinct to see a man shuffling through the door holding a stick. He wore a blue coat and a brown flat cap on his head, and although he was a little slow on his feet, his tone was bright and cheerful as he said, "Good morning!" There was a Midlands twang to his voice, and while he wasn't addressing anyone in particular, the owner and the two other people in the cafe besides us all replied, "Morning, George!" Even Nan looked up and smiled at him.

Clearly, he was popular in here.

"Hello, June," he said as he closed the door behind him. "How are you today, my darling?" He came around to stand at the side of the table, and Nan looked up from her drink.

"Not so bad, George," she said, though there was a distinct weariness in her tone that hadn't been there first thing. "How about you?"

"I'm all right. Just came in for a cup of tea before I go over to Teignmouth."

She nodded. "Do you want to join us?"

George waved his hand. "No, thank you, love. I'm waiting for a friend, but it's lovely to see you. Let's have a drink together next time."

Nan smiled. "Of course."

George gave us both a gentlemanly nod before heading over to a vacant table.

"He seems nice," I said, more to make conversation than anything else. I hadn't met any of her friends yet aside from Nova, although she had been out with them once or twice.

"He's lovely. I bet he was popular with the ladies back in the day." She stirred a spoonful of sugar into her tea as I poured my own drink.

"Seems pretty popular now," I said, as I saw him chatting to the other people in the cafe before he sat down. I could see what she meant, though. He was charismatic in his way, and everyone looked genuinely pleased to chat with him.

Nan chuckled. "Yeah. I see him in here quite often. Everyone loves George." As soon as the words were spoken, she stiffened a little, and her smile dropped.

"Are you okay?" I asked, watching her closely. I wasn't sure if she was unwell, and then her shoulders hunched and she leaned forward slightly. I was out of my seat in a second and rushed around the small table to crouch down beside her. "Nan? What's wrong?"

She took a deep breath but rested her hand over her chest. "I'm all right," she said. "I just... I don't know what I need."

Fear shot through me. Was she in pain? Was I about to lose another grandparent this year? Her face had paled, and my heart rate quickened. "Do you need me to call an ambulance?"

She shook her head. "No, no. Nothing hurts. I'm... I just don't feel..."

A trickle of relief filtered into my bloodstream, but something was obviously wrong.

"Do you want to go home?" I asked her.

"No. Not yet. I think I just..." Without warning, she burst into tears, covering her face with her hands. "I just miss him so much."

It was at that exact moment something shifted inside me.

I froze in my position, crouched beside her, and suddenly, she looked so small. So fragile. An array of memories flitted through my mind of her and Grandad coming to our house in Cornwall and hugging me tight, her smile wide. Grandad telling me silly jokes. Afternoons spent on the beach in Newquay, eating ice creams and paddling in the sea. Going to Nan and Grandad's house in Manchester for New Year, where we would stay up late listening to music and playing board games until the fireworks went off on the stroke of midnight. Times they had come to Italy, looking around at our home and being amazed at how light and spacious it was. They'd marvelled at the view, and Grandad teased her, saying he was going to leave her and move in with us.

Those were my memories. Short flashes that spanned twenty-eight years.

She was older now. Old and alone. And as content as she might have been day to day, she was still fighting her own battle to be okay in a world where the other half of her no longer existed.

Maybe that was what had felt so strange to me being around her again. I had nowhere near truly thought about the loss of my grandfather, but I realised I had never seen her without him. There was an imbalance, and while, obviously, I knew he was gone, it hadn't struck me that that was what had made everything off-kilter.

Or you did know, but you've been pretending you didn't see it.

I wasn't sure exactly what had set off this wave of grief in my nan, but I stood and dragged my chair close to hers, wrapping my arm around her and pulling her in close to me.

I swallowed down the lump in my throat and said, "It's okay, Nan. I've got you."

I rested my cheek against the top of her head, noticing George shooting an understanding smile across the cafe. I returned the smile as best I could, making sure never to loosen my hold on Nan.

This so wasn't the place for it. In public, with anyone likely to walk in at any time, but this cafe was friendly. Homely, hence the name. Even though Nan wasn't crying loudly, people had noticed, but they offered kind glances, then went on with their conversations, leaving us to it without judgement.

"Nan, I'm sorry," I whispered. "I'm really sorry."

"What for?" she asked, reaching up with one hand to wipe her cheeks.

"For not being here. For not calling. For being too busy with my own life that I didn't come back to see you and Grandad more often. Mostly, for not coming back for the funeral. And I'm not trying to make this about me, I'm just saying... I missed so much."

"Yes, you did," she said, but not unkindly. "But we never held it against you. We just wanted for you to be happy, and you were."

"Yeah, but for the last few months, you haven't been. And I wasn't here."

Nan pulled back slightly to look up at me. "Listen to me. I know I've been short with you at times. I've said some snappy things once or twice, mostly when you first got here, but it was a shock to see you. I *was* upset that you didn't come home for your grandad's funeral and I know you don't want to be here now, not really. But that doesn't mean I don't want you here. Your grandad and me, we love you very much, Donovan. More than you know. What matters is that you *are* here now."

Her words were more than fair, but they still hit me hard. To hear her say what I already knew was painful, but well-deserved. I hadn't made a secret of not wanting to go back to Dawlish. Or at least, I hadn't pretended I was excited to spend Christmas with someone who needed to not be lonely eating a Christmas dinner on her own, with Grandad's empty chair beside her.

The thing was, as I'd got to know her, I found I *did* want to be there. Getting to know the woman I should already have known better than I did. In fact, it seemed I got some of my temperament from her in that we could both be a little grumpy at times. She was way more naturally friendly than me, but there were definite similarities between us. I realised I wanted to know more about her past. Not just the years I missed, but things from before I was born. I didn't know how she had met my grandad, or what my mum was like as a child. Nan was a woman with a lifetime of stories I'd never bothered to read, and the guilt pounded at me in unrelenting waves.

"This is going to sound silly," Nan said, straightening up more but taking my hand. "This morning, I was thinking about all the bits and pieces I need to do to get ready for Christmas, and every year, your grandad would insist on making sure we had the pigs in blankets in early because they were his favourite thing on a Christmas dinner. And I've been so busy that I forgot to get them. I went to tell him I would get them today, like he was still here. Because every year, he would go on and on about it until I had them. And I got upset. I tried to pretend it was fine. That I wasn't just trying to talk to my dead husband in the kitchen even though he's long gone. And then, when we were sitting here, I got thinking about how your grandad loved a toasted teacake and it's... it's one of those harder days. They happen now and again, and it's extra hard now because this is the first Christmas without him."

Another fact I'd known but the impact hadn't fully hit me all the way just yet. Until then.

"I promise you won't be on your own this Christmas," I told her.

"Thank you, my love." She gave my hand another squeeze, and an idea came to me. "I'm seeing Nova this afternoon, but before that... please can we go to Grandad's grave?"

Tears welled in Nan's eyes again, and she nodded. "Yes," she said croakily. "We can."

WITHIN TWO HOURS, WE WERE BACK AT NAN'S HOUSE AFTER VISITING the cemetery and freshening up the flowers that had been left for him. Seeing his headstone brought home how real it all was, and Nan and I stood there for a while, holding hands in our own contemplative silence. Once again, memories drifted in and out of my mind, but regret was what weighed the heaviest. I'd loved growing up in Italy, but it had meant I left some of my family behind way earlier than most people usually would. And because of that, I'd wanted to see more of the world. No thoughts for anyone besides my parents.

When my paternal grandfather died when I was so young, it had thrown me off balance. Made me not want to be so close to anyone because losing him had been so fucking painful. Perhaps, without even fully realising I was doing it, I'd kept my distance from my maternal grandparents because I didn't want to experience that pain again. Maybe that was why I'd never wanted to settle down with someone. Although... I really had loved Paige. Would maybe have wanted to marry her and make a home somewhere eventually, but the timing was all wrong.

Or maybe timing was an excuse.

Honestly, it was impossible to know now. Maybe she just wasn't the right person.

The sound of the doorbell broke me out of my thoughts, and I knew it would be Nova, ready for our next task. I was meant to be going to her house for it, but since Nan wasn't doing so well, I'd asked Nova to come to us instead. I'd briefly explained what had happened in a text, and when I answered the door to her, she said, "Hey. How is she doing?" She stepped in, carrying yet another tote bag, this one with Disney princesses on the front.

"Better. Not great."

"And you?" she asked, looking up at me in a way that suggested she wasn't going to accept anything but the truth. Her brown eyes held concern. Genuine concern for me, even though I knew her thoughts about my lack of contact with my grandparents over the years. Like she had the other day, she'd seen there was more beyond the walls I kept around me. While it would usually have bothered me that someone had looked so closely, with her, it was okay. She wasn't just paying lip service; she actually cared. It might have been more for Nan than me, but she'd taken the time to ask about me, and I appreciated it.

I sighed. "I'm okay. Today was eye-opening. I'm still processing it all."

She nodded, and my answer seemed to satisfy her. With everything that had happened earlier, I'd forgotten I'd called her beautiful the night before. Looking at her now, dressed super casually in blue jeans and an oversized white jumper with black ankle boots, her hair scrunched back in a messy ponytail, she still looked beautiful. No tiredness or signs of a hangover from her night out and sleepover.

"Did you have fun last night?" I asked her.

She smiled. "I did. A night with the girls was just what I needed." She looked right into my eyes for a second, and as if remembering my message to her, her cheeks flushed slightly.

In order to not make a big deal out of it, I gestured towards the kitchen, and she followed me through and put the bag on the countertop before taking off her boots as she always did, then headed into the living room, where Nan was sitting on the sofa, doing a crossword in a magazine.

"Hey," Nova said brightly, and Nan looked up, smiling when she saw her.

"Hello, love," she answered. "I thought the two of you had plans this afternoon."

"We do, but we're going to do them here instead. I was wondering, if Donovan doesn't mind, if you want to join us."

"I don't mind," I said from the doorway. "What are we doing?"

Nova turned around to grin at me. "Making cookies."

I laughed. "When you said 'Keep it sweet', I was hoping it meant eating sweet things."

"Well, we can eat them afterwards," she pointed out. She turned back to Nan. "What do you say, June? Do you want to help?"

Although she looked a little worn out from the emotion of the day, she nodded. "Yes. I think I will."

Nova smiled at me over her shoulder as Nan stood up, and I stepped back into the kitchen to wait for them. "It's just as well," Nova said as they joined me. "It's been a long time since Donovan and I baked together, so we need some adult supervision." She grinned, and Nan laughed.

"You're probably right," I said. "I remember flour going everywhere and Mum complaining we were too messy."

"And yet still joining in," Nova added with a raised eyebrow.

That was my mum. She was, in many ways, a free spirit. Someone who let me just be who I was without trying to change anything about me or force me to be a certain way because *she* didn't like to be forced into being something she wasn't either. She was a mother and a wife, but she also worked hard and played harder. She never neglected the things she had to do, but once they were done, she was damn sure she was going to have a good time. Nobody had ever embodied living life to the fullest more than my mother, and I loved her for it.

"I would have tanned your backsides for making so much mess," Nan said sternly, but a smile still slipped through. She couldn't help it. After all, she was the one who had raised my mum, so she knew full well what life with her was like.

"I can believe that," Nova said, chuckling. She went to the table to pick up her bag of supplies and began unpacking them on the countertop. Sugar, flour, a carton of six eggs, butter, salt, icing sugar, food dyes, and baking powder. Then she dipped her hand into the bag and pulled out some cookie cutters in the shape of a gingerbread man, a Christmas tree, a candy cane, and a star. She turned back to Nan. "I'm hoping you have mixing bowls and baking trays. If not, I'll run back to the house."

"I have everything you need," Nan said, and she fixed her gaze on me. "Bottom cupboard in the corner. Go and get them, and I'll get the rolling pin."

"Hold on," Nova said. "There are two more things we need to do."

I couldn't help thinking she was enjoying this way too much as she reached into the bag and pulled out a thin pile of brightly coloured folded material. She giggled as she handed one piece to me and one to Nan, keeping the third for herself.

"What's this?" I asked with slight trepidation, hoping my guess was wrong. The hope was pointless. I knew exactly what this was, and as I held on to a string, I let the material unfold.

Yup. An apron. It was bright red with an upright reindeer body on it, the idea being that when I put it on, my head would be in the place the reindeer's should have been. I gave her a mock glare. "Please, please be kidding."

"Uh-uh." She shook her head, opening out her own apron to reveal a Santa body on hers, and she slipped it over her head, tying the strings behind her back. "This is part of the deal."

"I did not agree to dressing up like a tw... twit," I corrected myself, and Nan shot me a disapproving look while Nova snorted.

"Put your pinny on," Nan said, opening hers out and finding the body of a fairy in a pink dress on the front. "Unless you want this one?"

Nova threw her head back, and I assumed she was imagining me in that one instead.

"You are both evil." Still, I put my apron on, Nova watching me with amusement.

"Shall we take a photo for your blog?" she teased, raising an eyebrow.

I really needed to put some new content on there soon. I had scheduled a couple of things in advance, but after I'd posted that I was in Devon, I'd set those posts to hidden until a later date, knowing they would no longer make sense. I'd only posted once more since the post that had set Nova on this Christmas hit list thing, and I usually posted a couple of times a week. I'd also neglected my TikTok since I'd been in Dawlish. I'd been in to watch and like things and reply to comments, but I hadn't put up anything new in a while. Typically, I always went quiet on TikTok around Christmas and people understood I needed some downtime from new content now and again. Somehow, though, I thought if I posted a photo of me in a reindeer apron, my entire reputation as a moody asshole would be ruined.

"Maybe not for the blog," I said. "But I'm not against taking one just for us."

As much as a lot of my travels were online, I wasn't a big fan of selfies, and it hadn't occurred to me to take a photo with my nan yet. But this would be a good one to pick me up on days when I needed cheering up.

"Bring it in," Nova said, beckoning Nan and me towards her. She pulled her phone from the pocket of her jeans, and we all squeezed in together while Nova stretched her arm as far as she could to get us all in the frame. "Smile!"

God, she's cheesy. But it wasn't annoying on her. Her enthusiasm for simple things entertained me. She continued to thaw the coldness inside me, and I wasn't even sure how she was doing it. After Paige, anyone who made me feel that way was subtly extracted from my life. It was different with Nova because... she didn't feel new to me. It was like reuniting with an old friend and not like she was someone who was trying to wedge herself into my life. More that she was inviting me into hers. When it was time to leave after Christmas, I wouldn't stay away from England for anywhere near as long as I had before. I had more than one reason to come back now.

Nova took the photo while I shook that thought from my head. When she was done, she sent the photo to me and then began to scroll through her phone.

"I know I was trying to revive some of our Christmas traditions," she said, looking at me. "But one of mine and my mum's is to play Christmas music while baking. So, I'm adding that to the mix." She pressed play, and the sound of *Jingle Bell Rock* blasted out into the kitchen.

"Ooh, I love this one," Nan said, bopping her head to the beat.

Nova put her phone on the table out of the way of the mess we were about to make and then took hold of Nan's hands. "Then let's dance!"

Nova and Nan swung each other around the kitchen, both of them laughing and singing along, and yet another slab of ice dropped away from inside me. This was it. The thing Nova was trying to make me remember. The silliness and fun that could be had. I leaned against the counter, watching them, soaking up the happiness exuding from both of them. Nan had sobbed on my shoulder in the cafe. She hadn't been right all day, but Nova had swept in and given her a reason to smile again.

And it was fucking beautiful.

"Come on, Donovan," Nan said, letting go of one of Nova's hands and extending hers out to me. "You are never too old for a dance."

The me from a week ago would have rolled my eyes and made some sarcastic remark, but looking at my grandmother and feeling the love and peace she had in that moment, I couldn't say no. I pushed off of the countertop and took her hand in one of mine, taking Nova's hand with the other. She gave me a wink as our eyes met, and I grinned down at her and squeezed her hand. I didn't need to thank her for this moment. I knew she got it from the way her gaze softened, and I was sure I saw a brief sheen of tears in her eyes.

OKAY, YOU CHRISTMAS-LOVING WEIRDO. YOU WIN THIS ROUND.

CHAPTER 11

NOVA

Baking was a success. In a couple of hours, once we were all tidied up and June had gone upstairs for a nap, Donovan and I sat in her living room on the sofa with a hot chocolate each and the plate of cookies we'd made on the coffee table in front of us. It had been a fun afternoon spent laughing and dancing as we worked. Seeing June and Donovan bonding filled me with delight. Whether he wanted to admit it or not, he was definitely coming around to the idea of being around his family, and June needed it too. That connection. It had broken my heart to hear she'd been upset earlier. The idea of her breaking down in the cafe made me wish I'd been able to be there like I had so many other times. The most important thing, though, was she wasn't on her own for now. I always worried about her, and I called or text her every day or two if I didn't physically go to see her, just to make sure she was okay. Now, I didn't have to. Not that it had stopped me messaging or visiting. I just felt better knowing someone was with her.

"So, that was fun," I said, reaching over for a star-shaped cookie topped with white icing and snapping off a small piece.

Donovan nodded. "It was. Hopefully, these are more edible than the ones we used to make."

Smiling, I popped the piece I'd broken off into my mouth. The sugary sweetness was divine, and I gave a thumbs-up, making him laugh. He reached over for a Christmas tree-shaped cookie covered in green icing and those little silver edible ball things. Our design skills had improved since we were kids too.

"Thank you for what you did today," he said. "Nan had a rough day, and you really cheered her up." He took a bite of his cookie, letting out a small moan of approval. The sound made me chuckle.

"It's fine," I told him, breaking off another piece of my star. "I love June, and if there is any way I can make her feel better, I'll do it."

Before either of us could speak again, I heard a faint ringing sound from somewhere in the room. It sounded like an iPad, and I glanced at Donovan. His eyes darted around the room, and then he leapt up and crossed to the armchair June sat in sometimes—the one her husband used to sit in. Just peeking out from under a cushion, the corner of the device poked out and the screen was lit up. Donovan pulled it out.

"It's Nan's," he said. "And that is my parents trying to call her."

He swiped to answer it, then sat back down on the sofa while it connected. I wasn't in the frame, but I glanced over at the screen, curious to see what his parents looked like now.

"Oh!" Donovan's mum, Louise, said, her eyes widening in surprise. "Hi, darling!" She was sitting on what I assumed was a bed with Donovan's dad, Sam, beside her. It looked like they were in their cabin on the cruise ship.

"Hi," Donovan said, smiling. "Are you having fun?"

"We are!" Louise beamed, and I couldn't help smiling at her excitement. She looked just as I remembered her. She had thick black hair that hung way past her shoulders, and blue eyes not unlike Donovan's. His dad had much less dark hair on his head than he used to, and he wore glasses now, but to me, he didn't look much different either. "Alaska is just stunning."

"The ship's not bad either," Sam added with a grin that looked just like Donovan's when he was teasing me.

"I should bloody hope it's not bad for the price you paid," Donovan said, laughing. "Are you taking lots of photos?"

"We are," Louise told him. "I think your readers would love to see this place. You should do the trip. You'd love it."

"Alaska is on my list, but I think I want to go somewhere warm next, after I've been to see you."

The idea of him leaving made an unwelcome chill run through me. I wasn't sure why, though. I mean, this was how it had always been every time I'd known him. He came for the holidays, and then he left. The difference was, as a kid, I'd been okay with that. Understood he had to go. He had to go to school just like I did. Now... he didn't have any commitment to be in a certain place for a set amount of time. He did, however, have a job to do. One that paid him well to do what he loved.

Stop it. There is literally no reason for him to stay here, and you knew full well he was going to leave.

And I did know. But I wasn't done getting to know him yet.

Louise's smile widened. "We can't wait to see you and have you back at home."

"I can't wait to see you either." Donovan's eyes were so full of fondness for his parents that it took a little of the edge off about him going away. After all, what I'd wanted was for him to remember how important family was, and he was.

"Where's your nan?" Louise asked. "We've been trying to get through for days, but the wi-fi is unreliable out here, and with the time difference, it's been hard to reach her."

"She's just gone for a nap. She's had a bad day today." Donovan explained what had happened that morning, and I could see his mum getting emotional at the idea of her mother being so upset.

"We should have cancelled this trip and come home," Louise said, blinking away tears.

Sam wrapped an arm around her. "You know your mum would never have let you do that. She knows it's been hard for you too and she wanted you to come on this cruise."

She nodded, and Donovan said, "Mum, please don't worry. I'm here with her. She'll be fine."

"How are the two of you getting along?" Louise asked. "I hope you've been taking care of her."

Donovan rolled his eyes. "Of course I have. Although, I did sprain my ankle, which slowed me down a bit."

"How did you manage that?" Sam asked, and Donovan's eyes shifted to me for a moment. I grinned, waiting for him to explain.

Donovan chuckled and ran his hand through his hair. "I've actually got something to tell you. You aren't going to believe this."

"What is it?" Louise asked, brow raised with curiosity.

"So... do you remember when we used to come to Dawlish for Christmas when I was a kid, and I made friends with the girl who lived next door to Grandad?"

Louise said, "I remember. You used to sulk every time we left because you didn't want to leave her behind."

I covered my hand with my mouth to suppress my giggle as Donovan's cheeks reddened, and he closed his eyes as if he were trying not to die from embarrassment.

Instead of saying anything, he turned the iPad towards me, and I grinned, offering them a wave.

Louise's eyes widened again. "Nova?"

I nodded. "Hi!"

"Oh my goodness!" she breathed, shaking her head in shock.

Sam gaped. "Well, I'll be damned!"

"How did this happen?" Louise asked, and Donovan turned the iPad back to him, but he beckoned me closer, and I slid across the sofa to sit beside him so I was in the frame too.

"I live next door to your mum," I told her, laughing.

"So, you used to live next door to my dad, and now you live next to Lou's mum?" Sam asked. "Wow."

"I know. It's so weird. I couldn't believe it when Donovan and I realised we know each other."

Louise was still shaking her head, but she was smiling now. "So, how did this lead to a sprained ankle?"

Donovan looked at me, and said, "Yeah, that's all you. You can explain that one!"

I grinned up at him before telling Louise and Sam all about the Christmas hit list, and how we'd gone ice skating. I also told her about the movies we'd watched and our baking afternoon with June.

Louise howled with laughter at the idea of Donovan dancing in the kitchen, and Donovan nudged me with his shoulder when I pulled out my phone and showed her the photo of us in our Christmas-themed aprons.

"This is the best thing I've ever heard," she said. "I wish I'd been there to see that."

"Me too," I told her. "I'm just glad June was here or I doubt anyone would believe it happened."

"Yeah, all right," Donovan said, playfully shoving me away. "That's enough out of you."

I leaned away from him, laughing, but I caught Louise wiggling her eyebrows at him when she thought I wasn't looking. He glared back at her, but he was smiling as he did it, and it warmed my insides. I wasn't sure what the hell was happening here, but I liked it. Liked seeing Donovan so loosened up and talking to his parents again. It brought me back to my thoughts from before about where we would be if we'd had more Christmases together. About what could have happened if we hadn't been separated.

I wasn't a big believer in fate, but it was truly crazy that I had wound up living next door to both sets of Donovan's grandparents over the years. Especially when June and Trevor hadn't always lived in Devon. They had settled here, and yes, there was a family connection, but it wasn't their hometown like it was mine. I too had gravitated back there, even though it made more logical sense for me to live closer to my parents and work.

Was there a reason we had found each other, or was it purely a bizarre coincidence?

Zoning back into Donovan's chat with his parents, I realised they were saying goodbye, and I focused my attention back on the screen, moving a little closer to him again so I was fully back in the frame.

"Nova, honey, it was lovely to see you again," Louise said. "When we're over at Easter, we'll have to have a catch-up."

"I'd love to," I said sincerely. "We can go out for lunch or something."

"It's a date!"

Once the goodbyes were said, my cheeks hurt from smiling so much, and Donovan placed the iPad on the coffee table, behind our plate of now-forgotten cookies.

"So, you used to sulk when you left me, huh?" I teased, tilting my chin upwards. We were still sitting close beside each other, and he stiffened for just a second before relaxing.

"Fuck off," Donovan said, laughing. "I will kill my mother for saying that."

"In her defence, she didn't know I was here."

"True."

I thought back to those days. When he and his family would leave three or four days after Christmas, and I'd spend the rest of the holiday on my own. Considering we had hardly known each other, once he was gone, I somehow felt like I was missing a limb until I went back to school and real life resumed. Playing with my new toys was hollow when he wasn't around to share them with.

"Well, if it helps, I sulked after you left too," I told him.

He grinned. "Yeah?"

"Yup. But only for a little while. Once I dived into playing with my presents and eating my Christmas chocolates, I was over it."

I laughed out loud as he scowled at my lie, but as I went to move back to my side of the sofa, he wound his arm around my shoulder, keeping me in place. I looked up at him, and his eyes met mine, soft but serious.

When he didn't speak, I softly said, "I always wondered what had happened to you. I mean, not *always*, but for a long time. A lot of Christmases. I didn't know back then, when I first knew you, that anything might change. That I wouldn't see you again, and when it happened, I was upset."

He nodded. "I was too. When I went back to my grandad's and you weren't next door, I didn't know what I would do for the holidays. I wondered where you were and if you were still doing the same things with new friends."

"I wasn't. Not for a few years, anyway. Every Christmas you weren't around, I missed you. But I realised eventually you wouldn't think about me anymore. We were just kids, and we were both growing up and doing different things. So, I made new traditions with my new friends. I have always thought about you every time I watched *Home Alone*, though."

I smiled, but he didn't. His face remained serious. "After Grandad died... the first one you lived next door to, I shut down. I wanted to forget everything about Dawlish because it was too painful. Christmas made me think of him, and you were so intertwined with that, I set those memories aside. It was easier to forget when we went to Italy. I didn't realise how much I'd forgotten until you reappeared in my life."

"Well," I said quietly, "I hope me being around again is not all bad."

He shook his head. "It's not bad at all."

Our gaze remained connected, and I was very aware his arm was still around me, his hand resting high on my shoulder. It felt... familiar somehow. I wanted to touch him too, but I also wasn't sure what was happening. Whether we were having a moment of fond reminiscing or if it was something more.

"I meant what I said last night," he said. "You really did look beautiful. You always look beautiful."

The butterflies that had been softly flitting around in my tummy picked up their pace, and I drew in a sharp breath at the intensity.

Slowly, I reached forward, resting my hand on his shoulder, my thumb lightly stroking a tiny bit of the exposed skin close to his neck. My eyes dropped to his lips before shifting back to meet his gaze again.

He moved his head just a fraction closer before his lips met mine in the softest kiss I'd ever experienced. His lips against mine stirred the butterflies in my stomach again, and I closed my eyes, taking in each second of this new connection between us. He tasted sweet, like the cookies we'd been eating, and I wanted more of this. Of him.

He slid his hand down my arm, then let it rest on my waist, gently moving me closer. Breaking the kiss for a moment, he softly said, "Come here."

He placed his other hand on my side, guiding me onto his lap so I was straddling him, my knees on either side of his thighs. I didn't have time to think as he moved a hand around to the back of my neck and pulled me in to kiss him again, his scruffy beard occasionally tickling my chin. I wound my arms around his neck, relishing in the slow dance of our lips moving together to a silent beat.

What are you doing?

The question hit me like a lightning bolt, but I couldn't stop kissing him. Being pressed against him, his firm chest close to mine… it felt so comfortable. So *right*.

Whatever reasons I had for not giving into any kind of feelings for him, they didn't compare to the sheer bliss of being close to him. Not just physically, either. Something had changed in him over the past few days. Something that had allowed me to slip through some of his defences. He laughed more, frowned less. His mood was lighter, and it was as if he was letting me get to know the real him. The man behind the moody blogger he portrayed online.

But the physical part was pretty freaking great too.

His hands slid down my back, tightening around me, and a small sigh escaped my lips as I pulled back slightly to look at him. His eyes were dark with what looked like lust, and the memory of Gaby saying something similar caused me to swallow back a giggle.

"What just happened?" I asked, remaining pressed against him.

He twisted his lips to the side as if thinking hard about the question. "I think I kissed you."

"Ohhh," I said, nodding over-exaggeratedly. "It's been a while. I'd forgotten what that felt like."

Donovan smiled, and I matched it with one of my own. "I'd really like to do that again."

"Me too, but…" I trailed off, unsure what my next words were. Was there even a but? I knew all the reasons I'd decided nothing could happen between us, but now it had. And I liked it. Liked his hands on my back and his lips on mine.

"Would you like to go on a date with me tonight?"

His words broke the train of overthinking I'd been about to hop on, and I said, "Tonight?"

"Yeah." He brushed his lips against mine again.

"What did you have in mind?"

"What would you like to do? Dinner? A movie?" He paused, knowing there weren't many date places close by.

After considering his question for a moment, I said, "There is something on our list we could do that might be a bit date-like."

He raised an eyebrow. "Late night cruising?"

"Yeah. It doesn't have to be late; it just needs to be dark. Maybe we could go and grab a drink somewhere after."

"Sounds like a plan to me. What time do you want me?"

Now.

I shook the thought away, but my cheeks heated anyway. "About seven? I'll drive because I know where I want to go."

"Okay. That works for me."

A wave of heady joy mixed with trepidation, arousal, and shock washed over me all at once, and I wanted to launch myself at him and run away at the same time. Unable to decide, I leaned into him, resting my forehead on his shoulder as overwhelm took over me.

This was a lot. One minute, we'd been talking to his parents, and the next, I was on his lap, and we were joined at the lips. I was trying to pretend every part of my body wasn't aching to be closer to him, inhaling the scent of cookies, hot chocolate, and his usual aroma of... whatever body wash he used. It was cool fresh, and sexy.

Donovan tightened his arms around me, and I snuggled closer, allowing him to make me feel safe, even though there was nothing safe about the way I felt in that moment.

"This is scary for me too," he said, one hand slowly rubbing up and down my back. "I didn't..." he trailed off.

I wanted to ask what he was going to say but was unsure if I would like his answer, so I let it go. The fact he understood my trepidation was oddly reassuring. It wasn't a bad kind of scary; not for me, anyway. It was more that it was unexpected. Not even that. It was that it *should* have been unexpected, but it wasn't. Something seemed to have drawn us together. The connection had been simmering since the day he walked back into my life, and now there was no way to go back. To pretend it wasn't there and we were merely two people hanging out.

I lifted my head to look at him. His blue eyes held a sparkle as they met mine, and I felt like I'd just had my first kiss. "What are we doing, Donovan?"

He moved his hand up a little more, burying it in my hair. I closed my eyes as his fingers tenderly teased the long strands. "Do we have to answer that right now? Because all I want to do at the moment is just be with you. Like this."

With lines like that, he was going to kill me. There was no hope, no way to defend myself when his words were melting me into a gigantic puddle of slush.

"We don't have to answer right now," I said a little breathily, opening my eyes again. "Please, just kiss me again."

The slow smile on his lips made my heart beat faster. "I can do that."

CHAPTER 12

DONOVAN

WRAPPED IN MY THICK BLACK COAT, A SCARF AROUND MY NECK AND wearing my thickest jeans and boots, I left Nan's house to meet Nova for our date.

I'd asked Nova on a date.

I'd also spent most of the afternoon with her on my lap, kissing her, and it was the best fucking afternoon I'd had in ages.

Was I right to kiss her knowing I wouldn't be staying around for much longer? Maybe not. But I couldn't help it. The time I'd spent with her was showing me I could still care about people, and that day, I'd seen her take my nan from heavy with grief to light and relaxed with just an apron, some Christmas music, and a lot of cookies. When Nova had sat chatting with my parents as easily as if they had never lost contact, I knew I was screwed.

Gorgeous, kind, unassuming, sweet... I'd just wanted to be close to her. And now we were going on a date. I wasn't sure why I was so nervous about it. Maybe because I hadn't been on an actual first date in three years. Some of that was due to the global pandemic, most of which I'd spent in New Zealand, but even since then, there hadn't been a single person I'd wanted to take out. I'm not going to pretend there weren't a couple of one-nighters along the way, but as for dating... there had been nothing.

I was about to head down Nova's path when she opened the front door and stepped out. She was wearing a long black coat buttoned all the way to the top and those damn knee-highs again. She also wore a black hat with a bobble on the top, which would be needed in the almost zero-degree temperature. It had been unbearably and unusually cold for the last couple of weeks, but I was getting used to it now.

Nova smiled as she walked towards me, her keys in her hand occasionally glinting as they caught the glow of the streetlights.

"Hey," she said as she reached me, where I stood just beside her car.

The pause was awkward. We'd spent all afternoon kissing, but we weren't exactly together, and yet this was a date. Was I meant to kiss her in greeting? Did she expect me to?

Get your fucking shit together, you dick.

I leaned down and lightly pressed my lips to hers. "Hi."

She smiled up at me, the now-familiar blush on her cheeks. "Shall we get going?"

"Sure."

Once we were in the car, Nova started it up, making sure the heater was on, and I said, "Do I get any clues as to where we're going?"

She shook her head. "Nah. I'll just drive. I'm sure you'll figure it out."

She turned out of our street onto John Nash Drive, a name I'd learned after getting the town bus with Nan several times when I was unable to drive. The long street was deserted, aside from one man walking a dog. His pace was quick, like he was in a rush to get out of the cold, and he puffed out wisps of breath as he hurried along.

"Is your nan okay?" Nova asked, glancing at me.

"Yeah. The nap did her good, and she seemed much brighter when she woke up."

Nova nodded. As I glanced at her profile, I knew what she was thinking. The rigidity in her shoulders told me exactly what was on her mind. Of course it was. It had been on my mind too when Nan had woken up. Did I tell her what happened with Nova, or just say nothing for now? It was a very short debate since I didn't know where any of this was going.

"She doesn't know we kissed, but she does know we're going out for a drink and not just one of your Christmas tasks," I told her.

She nodded again. "It's really helpful that you know what I'm thinking without me asking." A grin crossed her face. "I wasn't sure if that was a weird question."

"It's not weird. I didn't know whether to tell her either. I just told her you'd spoken to Mum and Dad and that you and I decided to go out tonight."

"What did she say?"

"You know what she's like." I smirked, even though Nova wasn't looking at me. "She just told me to have fun, but with that knowing look in her eyes."

Nova laughed. "I know the look. My mum gave me the same look when I was leaving her house the other day."

Ohh. That was why she was blushing the day we went there to pick up the crutches.

"Speaking of my mum," she said. "She called a little while ago because, before you arrived, she asked me if your nan would want to spend Christmas Day with us. Since you got here, though, I assumed Mum had realised June wouldn't be coming. But Mum has now asked if both of you want to join us. I was going to ask your nan, but I also wanted to see how you would feel about it too."

I raised my eyebrows. Christmas with just me and Nan was what I'd been expecting. I'd also expected it to be quiet and fairly depressing. Her first Christmas without Grandad was never going to be a bundle of laughs, and it was one of the reasons I'd originally intended to leave right after Boxing Day. But if we were to spend it with Nova...

The idea made me... excited?

Not in the way I'd been when she was sitting on my lap earlier, but in a way I hadn't experienced since I was a kid. Like something incredible was about to happen and anything was possible. It was a rush of seasonal joy I was sure had long since left me, and it made me laugh out loud with surprise.

"Bad idea?" Nova asked, her eyes remaining on the road.

"No!" I said, wanting to quickly clear up any misunderstanding. "That wasn't why I was laughing. I think it's a good idea. Do you want me to ask Nan, or do you want to do it?"

"Up to you. Are you sure you'd be okay with it? If you'd prefer to spend it just the two of you, I totally understand."

I knew she would, but the tiny glimmer of hope in her eyes that we would spend the day with her family did something to my gut. It wasn't just about me. She adored my nan, and I think a part of her wanted Nan to be surrounded by as many people as possible to ensure she didn't feel alone.

And all that did was make me like her more.

"I think it would be great for us all to be together for Christmas," I said. "I'll ask her tonight and let you know."

"Mum also said you can both stay the night because she has plenty of room. I'm staying over anyway, and it means you can have a drink if you want to."

Easy to see where she gets her thoughtfulness from. Nova's mum, Anita, was always so kind. Not as over-the-top excitable as my own mother, but still always fun. Her dad, Oliver, was quiet, from my recollection. Friendly, but much more introverted than my dad. It would be nice to see them again, and offering for us to stay over was especially kind of them. I wasn't sure Nan would go for the sleepover, but I thought she might like to at least spend the day with the McKays.

I grinned. "Are we too old to sleep in the same room now?" I teased, then taking it a step further, I added, "I noticed you never put sleepovers on the list."

"Ha ha," she said, trying to sound stern but failing and breaking into a laugh. "We only ever had one sleepover when we were kids. Plus, I thought you were unbearable when I wrote our list. I didn't want to spend *that* much time with you!"

Leaning my head back against the headrest, I chuckled. "How about now?"

She shrugged with fake nonchalance. "You're all right, I suppose."

"I'll take that."

Snorting out a laugh, she reached over and turned on the car radio, and Christmas music played softly. It was only then I looked up and realised where we were.

"Are we doing the Christmas lights tour?" I asked as we ascended the hill onto Coronation Avenue, a street that had once been renowned for having the best lights in town. Grandad Cain told me that they used to hold a carol concert outside one of the family's houses to raise money for charity, but I'd never got to see it myself.

"We are," Nova replied. "I do this every year, but I haven't had a chance yet. So, I thought this might be a good thing to do since your dad always used to take us on this drive."

I looked around at the Christmas lights that adorned windows and the light-up reindeer and snowmen in people's front gardens. Not all of the houses were decorated the way they used to be, but there was still plenty to look at.

Nova and I used to sit in the back of my dad's car, pointing out the best displays and getting excited when we saw something especially impressive. My mum sat in the front seat, singing her head off to Christmas music, and Nova would giggle at her tuneless wailing. The memory made me smile.

"Do you remember the time my mum and dad tried to do a rendition of Fairytale *of New York*?" I asked, another long-buried memory springing into my head.

"Oh my God, yes!" Nova turned into another street I didn't know the name of, where the houses were bigger and the displays more exuberant.

"Probably a bit inappropriate with kids in the car now I think about it," I said.

"Eh, it's a classic."

She slowed the car right down, just like my dad used to, so we could look at the festive lights as we went by. Nova hummed along quietly to the music, and the glow of the bright lights seemed to make her delight at seeing them shine even brighter.

Fuck, she's pretty.

And I'd kissed her. And was maybe going to spend Christmas with her.

Calm the fuck down. She's just a woman.

A woman who was breaking me. I'd gone from not wanting to be involved in anything traditionally Christmassy and getting the hell out of town as soon as possible to enjoying the things I used to love and wanting to be around Nova more.

It had been an odd day all around. From Nan's breakdown, to baking, to talking to my parents, kissing Nova, and now this drive. I felt a little out of control, but not in a bad way. Usually, I planned things. I had to in order to get to where I needed to be next, and when I'd got back to Dawlish, I was irritated that I hadn't yet chosen where my next destination would be. I knew I would return to Italy when my parents got back there, though I hadn't intended to stay in the UK until then. But I'd been swept up in doing things with Nan and Nova. Dealing with my own shit. And I still hadn't booked a flight anywhere.

I'd thought about spending a couple of weeks in France before going back to Italy, but I could just stay where I was. Not forever, but for a little longer.

A strange tension filled the car, like she'd heard my confused thoughts. She couldn't have known exactly where my mind was going, but she'd obviously sensed my shift in mood. Or maybe her own thoughts were equally confusing.

I didn't want it to be like this, though. I wanted it to be how it had been earlier. Relaxed, maybe a little cautious, but mostly just enjoying the moment we were in.

Unable to think of the words to break the tension, I just kept looking out of the window as Nova drove, and eventually, she circled us back to the end of Coronation Avenue, where she parked outside the last house on the street.

"Why are we here?" I asked, and she turned her head to look at me.

"I know it's freezing, but there's one more place I want to take you to. I'm not sure if you've ever seen this view before, especially at night and in December."

"Okay," I said. "I trust you."

The words were said with a hint of teasing because she had threatened my life more than once, and I was pretty sure we were headed to the cliff that overlooked the sea.

She laughed lightly, and we got out of the car. Once it was locked, we walked the short distance to the road which was, thankfully, quiet at this time of the evening. We crossed and headed up a small path that opened out into an expanse of grass and trees, a small path winding around the edge. Another path cut down the middle of the grassy area. The chill hit me since we were right by the sea now, and I reached over and took Nova's hand. She smiled up at me, her cold fingers squeezing around mine, and we headed to the railing that safeguarded people from tumbling down the red rocky cliffside.

"Here," she said, waving her free arm towards the view.

It was breathtaking. The darkness didn't hinder its beauty at all. The water was calm, just some gentle waves lapping at the sand, and way beyond, the lights from a town that curled into the distance. Turning my head, I looked towards what I could see of Dawlish. It wasn't much from where we were, but the Christmas lights attached to the streetlamps shone brightly, the occasional car slowly driving around the mini golf course which sat on a small island in the centre of the one-way road. There was a train just pulling out from the train station, and I watched as it disappeared on the long track towards Dawlish Warren.

"Fuck. I hadn't ever been up here before," I said. "I've been on the beach, of course, but never up here."

"I love it here. It's where I go to think. Well, I start here, then wander down to the beach. I'm sure the sea is the reason I can't stay away from this place. It's so relaxing."

"You know other places have beaches too, right?" I teased, and she stiffened for a second.

"This will always be my favourite."

I stepped around her, very carefully pressing her back against the railing, and looked at her in the moonlight, the incredible backdrop behind her making her look more stunning than ever. Moving in closer to her, I dropped her hand and slid my arms around her back, wishing our huge coats weren't in the way so I could really feel her warmth.

"I like it here," I told her, my gaze piercing hers, hoping she knew what I meant. Not just the scenery, but *her*.

She nodded, her arms snaking around my back. "Me too."

I leaned down as she tilted her head up, already loving how easily we fit together. How I knew what her lips tasted like, and how I wanted more of her kisses. More of everything that was her.

"Nova," I whispered against her neck. "Please can we just not overthink this?"

She tensed again, and as much as I wanted to pull back to see her face, I didn't. I anticipated the caution that would be in her eyes. She didn't want to get hurt, and I didn't want to hurt her. It told me this was dangerous for her because maybe she was already feeling more than she should so soon.

Yeah, and you're totally chill about this.

The sarcastic voice in my head was starting to piss me off because it was right. I felt it. I might have even felt it from the beginning. When she apologised for me spraining my ankle, even though it wasn't her fault. When I saw how much she cared for my grandmother. How much she wanted to look inside me and find something she recognised because, somehow, she knew it was still in there, even when I didn't.

"What if I'm already overthinking it?" she asked quietly.

This time, I did pull back a little, and the hesitance was right there, shining brightly like I knew it would be. I placed my hand on her cheek. "I can't make that stop. All I can do is be here. With you. For right now."

She swallowed hard as she looked up at me. "Live in the moment?"

I nodded. "Yeah. Live in the moment."

Her eyes softened a little. I knew she wasn't totally convinced, and if I wasn't such a self-centred piece of shit, I would have walked away from her before either of us got any more entangled with each other.

But I couldn't do it.

Without another word, she held me tighter, burying her head against my chest like she had earlier, and I wound my hand into her hair.

Home.

The word echoed in my head over and over as I held her. What did that even mean to me? I'd had so many it had lost its meaning over time. It had become a nothing. Something that held no meaning because I was always moving. Home had been a hostel, or a hotel room, or a short-stay rental apartment for years. The longest I'd stayed anywhere was during the pandemic, and only because I was forced. I loved New Zealand. I would always go back and visit, but that wasn't home either. Was it here? Was it Cornwall? Italy?

They were all places I'd lived growing up, but none of them were my *place*. Italy was maybe as close as it got, and then Nova appeared.

Her tucked against me had made a word I'd been so afraid of become real again.

Is home really ever a place? Had it ever been?

"I can hear you thinking as hard as I am," Nova said with a small laugh.

"Well, I never said you were the only one doing it. But... I just want to take this as it comes. One day at a time."

"Okay." She relaxed fully in my arms as she looked up at me. "We still have one more thing left on our list."

"Just one? That was fast."

"Yeah. Maybe I should have thought of some more."

"Or we could make new traditions."

She smiled. "Maybe we should."

I placed a kiss on her forehead. "Shall we go and get a drink now?"

"Sure. I'd like that."

Once we left the beauty of Lea Mount, something shifted again. A more relaxed air surrounded us, and we chatted easily over a couple of drinks at The Smugglers before heading back to Nova's place.

We sat outside in her car, the radio and heater still on to keep us warm, and it seemed as though neither of us wanted to move.

"Do you want to come in?" she asked, and as soon as the words left her lips, her face flushed.

She was so fucking adorable and sexy, and I laughed softly. There was nothing I wanted to do more than go inside with her. Snuggle up with her and then do all the things that had slowly begun to play out in my mind from the moment we first kissed. "Yes. I do. But... I think I should probably not. Not tonight."

I hoped the way I looked at her let her know it wasn't because I didn't want her. We both needed a moment to get used to what was happening. And I needed to ask Nan about Christmas Day with Nova's family.

She nodded, nothing but understanding on her features. "Okay. In that case, shall we head in?"

"Sure."

Nova turned the engine off, and we both got out of the car. She walked around to the path, where I waited for her so I could kiss her goodnight. She melted against me, holding me tight as I kissed her lips.

CHAPTER 13

NOVA

ONCE I WAS SAFELY INSIDE, CUP OF TEA IN HAND AS I SAT IN MY USUAL spot beside the glow of my Christmas tree lights, I let out a long sigh.

What a day.

Every part of it had been like a rollercoaster ride, my stomach leaping and dropping with each new twist. My head was still spinning.

Donovan had asked me if I could live in the moment with him. I'd always thought I was a live-in-the-moment kind of girl, but that wasn't totally true. Yes, I liked to do things I enjoyed when I could. As often as I could. But that never stopped concerns creeping in. What if something happened to my job? To my parents. What if I was destined to grow old alone? Never bring someone new into my family and experience what life would be like with the right person?

What if I got hurt?

That was the loudest voice right then. I was in serious fucking trouble.

I wasn't sure exactly how any of it had happened. One minute, he was some irritating man who was staying next door, the next he was someone I'd once been friends with. Someone I was now having fun with.

Someone I was so attracted to it scared the hell out of me.

I'd been okay with admitting he was attractive when I first saw him, but that was all I thought it would ever be; an appreciation of a handsome man. Now, though, however ill-advised, it was a struggle not to think about him. Not to touch him whenever he was close. When we'd first got into my car earlier, I'd still been a little on edge, but after talking to him, holding him on the clifftop, I knew the only thing I could do from now on was exactly what I'd agreed to. To take this thing a day at a time.

But can I really *do that?*

I held onto my cup of tea tightly, staring at the steam rising from the surface as if it might somehow hold the answers.

With a sudden flash of inspiration, I reached over to the end of the sofa where I'd dumped my phone and picked it up, scrolling through my contacts until I reached Gaby's number. I hit the button to call her, hoping she wasn't busy, and she answered within two rings.

"Hey, Nova! Missing me already?" she teased.

"Always," I told her, already brightened just from the sound of her voice.

She laughed. "What can I do for you, sweetheart? Everything okay?"

"Yeah, I just... I needed someone to talk to. About Donovan."

"Ooh," she squealed, and I could just picture her salivating at the idea of some gossip. "Did something happen?"

I gave her a brief rundown of the day's events, and when I'd explained the basics of it all, I said, "The thing is, Gabs, I don't know if I can just be casual with him. It's not like I'm in love and can't live without him. I definitely can't marry him," I mused, the thought hitting me out of nowhere. "His last name is Cain."

There was a pause while Gaby realised what I meant, then she howled with laughter. "Nova Cain! Oh my God, you have to marry him! Then you can have a daughter, and you can call her Candy!"

Her cackling laughter had deviated me from the seriousness, and I started to laugh with her. "Fitting since every interaction we've ever had has been at Christmas."

"See? It's meant to be."

"Piss off," I said, even though I was still laughing. "I have an actual problem here. And not just a ridiculous-for-me surname."

"I'm sorry." She snorted once more, then said, "Okay. Go on."

I inhaled deeply, trying to find the point I had been trying to make. "So, anyway... there's just something about him that's pulling me in. And I don't know if I should get closer to him when it's all going to end soon."

"Who says?" she asked.

"Out loud, nobody. But him leaving is something we both know is going to happen. It lurks between us, and it did from the first time he kissed me. It was like we crossed the line and now we can't go back."

"Do you want to? If you could take back today, would you?"

The question required no thought. "Nope. But it doesn't change how risky it is."

"Okay, well let me ask you this. How do you feel when you're with him?"

Blowing out a breath, I said, "Happy. Safe. Horny."

Gaby laughed out loud. "Ah, the three perfect things to feel for a man. And I'm guessing you like those things."

"I do. But I'm also aware those feelings will have nowhere to go when he disappears off to wherever he's going. Is it truly worth getting any more involved with him?"

"Nova, he's right next door. Say you call time on whatever this is tonight. Then what? He's there, and you know only a wall is separating you. You could bump into him anytime. How are you going to cope if you have him right there and you stop yourself from going near him?"

A small knot formed in my stomach, tightening at the idea of seeing him outside and then us going our separate ways. Even if that would be the end result after Christmas, more than a week of knowing he was my neighbour would kill me if I couldn't be with him.

But that was bad too. Because if I felt that way now, how would I feel when he was gone?

"I don't want to avoid him," I said. "I don't. I guess I'm just nervous about feeling too much. Or more than I already feel."

"The way I see it, darlin', it's too late to stop it now. The feelings have already happened. Whether you see him or you don't, you're going to hurt when he's gone. Why not just make the most of what you have while he's here?"

Something June said to me right after she lost Trevor drifted into my mind.

"If I could have just one more day with him. To say goodbye. To tell him I loved him. I would take any moment of time I could get with him, but it's too late."

This wasn't the same, of course. June was talking about the sudden loss of the man she had been with for most of her life. She hadn't had the chance to tell him the things she wanted to, even though he already knew them. She needed him to *know* she loved him... to say it once more, but she couldn't.

Donovan wasn't that to me. But he was someone I wanted to be around. And if a week was all we had left, if I could soak up the joy of being with him for as long as I could, why shouldn't I? Like Gaby said, the feelings were already there. That ship had sailed the second his lips met mine, so now, all I could do was go along for the ride.

"Gaby, this is why I love you," I said. "Thank you."

She laughed. "You didn't need my help. You just needed to talk it out."

"Yeah, I guess so. But thank you anyway. Do you wanna meet up before New Year? Maybe go out for some drinks in Exeter?"

"Oh, hell yeah! You're welcome to stay at mine."

"That would be great. Bring Shannen too. She's lovely."

"She is. I'll ask her and see if she's up for it."

After a quick round of goodbyes, I put my phone in my lap and took a sip of my rapidly cooling tea. Another night out with my friends would be just what I needed once Donovan had swept out of my life. If that was when he was leaving. He still hadn't specified a date, just that he was leaving sometime before his parents got home from their cruise, though he had said he could stay through some of

January. The idea warmed me a little, knowing it might not be over as soon as I'd thought.

My text tone went off, and I was fully expecting a reassuring message from Gaby. Instead, Donovan's name was on the screen.

> Nan says she would love for us to spend Christmas with you and your family. She also said to let her know if your mum needs anything bringing as she would like to contribute. I would too xx

I smiled and typed back:

> I'll ask her. I don't think she'll want anything, though. Unless we want to make some more cookies :p xx

After a few moments, he replied:

> I'm up for that. P.S. I miss you. xx

The goosebumps erupting on my skin at his message made me pull the sleeves of my jumper down over my hand. Not in a bad shivery way. In the best kind of way. Because I knew he meant it. And because I missed him too, even though we had been apart for less than an hour. In spite of all my concerns, I hadn't had anywhere near enough of him yet.

I answered:

> Come over. Please. xx

There was no need to wait for his reply. I knew in the depths of my soul he would be at my place soon. I could imagine him making up an excuse to June as to why he had to come back. Probably something about Christmas arrangements. I chuckled to myself as I placed my cup on the table.

Two minutes later, my phone vibrated with another text.

June
I'm not sure who my grandson thinks he's
fooling but it isn't me. Have fun my darlings
xxxxxx

The doorbell rang just as I giggled at the message. Standing, I hammered out a response.

Thank you, June. See you tomorrow xx

The buzzing anticipation of his arrival had been slightly broken by June's message, and when I opened the door to him, before he could say anything, I held my phone up to him to show him the text.

"Way to ruin the mood," he said, laughing and shaking his head.

"Yeah. But it's also kinda sweet."

He stepped inside, and I shut and locked the door behind him. "I suppose it is."

He didn't have his coat on since it took approximately twenty seconds to run to my house, and I slipped my phone into my jeans pocket as I looked up at him.

The crooked smile on his lips was both cute and hot as hell. An almost-smirk, but with a fondness shining from his eyes.

"So, you missed me, huh?" I asked, quirking an eyebrow at him.

"A little," he replied, feigning nonchalance.

"Hmm. Only a little. Seems a lot of effort to come back out in the cold if you only missed me a little."

His smile widened, and he put his hands on my waist, pressing me back against the wall. "I missed you loads," he said, his mouth covering mine in a kiss that knocked the breath out of me. I wound my arms around him, pulling him in closer, my hands clinging to the soft material of his dark green jumper that hugged his body perfectly.

If it wasn't for the fact I'd missed him too, I'd have thought he was just trying to butter me up. The truth was, even before we'd ever kissed, walking away from him had become harder, and each time I knew I would see him, my entire body felt more alive. I'd got the same

110

feeling from him earlier. The way he'd looked at me when he opened the door to me earlier; he'd seemed to brighten somehow. Not just his smile, but everything about him.

"I missed you too," I told him, capturing his lips with mine once more.

Donovan slid one hand down to my hip, while the other moved up, his fingers softly stroking the back of my neck. His touch on my bare skin made me tingle, and I closed my eyes at the sensation as his fingertips circled gently. Just the simple stroke was making me melt into him, against him, and I held him tighter as my heart began to race.

"You look so fucking perfect right now," he murmured, and when I opened my eyes, his were on me, darker than usual as he watched me.

"Donovan, I..." I trailed off, unsure what I was even trying to say.

My body reacted to the gentleness of his fingers as they continued to tease my skin, and I wanted so much more. But the speed of everything was making me dizzy.

Or maybe it was just him.

Gazes still connected, Donovan said, "We don't have to do anything more than this. I just want to be with you."

I nodded slowly. "What if I want more?"

He kissed me tenderly. "We can do that too." Another brush of lips. "But that isn't the reason I came over."

I wouldn't have believed any other man who said that to me. Usually, sex was always the reason. But I knew he meant it. It was clear from the way he was pressed against me he wanted me as much as I wanted him, but if all I had asked to do was curl up on the sofa and talk, he'd have been okay with it.

But that wasn't what I wanted.

I wasn't sure what the hell Donovan was doing to me, but any normal rules I had about sex on a first date were disappearing while his eyes burned into mine.

We'd had the best day. Bumpy in places, but all in all, it was a day I would happily have done all over again. Even the awkward parts, because it was real. Neither of us had any need to pretend to be anything other than who we were, and although things between us were undefined and complicated in so many ways, there was no way to pretend the chemistry between us wasn't there. It seemed to get stronger with every day to the point people could see it. First Gaby and Shannen, then Donovan's mum, and then June.

Live in the moment.

When it came down to it, that was all we ever had.

"What are you thinking?" Donovan asked, his hand drifting up to my cheek to gain my attention. I'd been looking at him the whole time, but he could tell I'd drifted away, trying to figure out what I wanted.

I lightly kissed his lips, my hands moving down his back to the waistband of his jeans. "I'm thinking I would really like you to stay with me tonight."

CHAPTER 14

DONOVAN

I AM IN SO MUCH FUCKING TROUBLE.

I lay beside Nova in her bed, watching her as she slept soundly. She was still wrapped around me, and my arms were around her, holding her as the morning sun peeked in through the curtains.

We'd fallen asleep like this. Naked, limbs entwined.

And it felt good. Waking up beside her felt good.

When she'd asked me to stay, it had been... surprising. I wasn't surprised she wanted me because that had been clear from the moment she opened the door to me, and I wanted her just as much. But I hadn't expected it to move so fast. She was unsure of what we were, and she was probably right to be. Nothing was clear, only that we liked each other.

And now I'd touched her. Seen all of her. Not just her body, but her heart, which I was pretty sure she was offering me with every kiss. Like a greedy bastard, I took it, but not without surrendering a piece of my own in return.

I really hadn't meant to. Not to take nor to give. I'd just wanted to be with her. Spend the night with her and live in the moment, just like we'd said.

I'd never thought of myself as a 'sex changes everything' kind of guy. Sex was sex. I hadn't had as many one night stands as I could have, but when I did, I never had a problem walking away.

This isn't a one-night stand, you moron.

I knew that before we'd walked up her stairs. Because a one-night stand didn't usually come with the strings already attached. I hadn't lied when I'd text her to say I missed her. It was the God's honest truth, and even though it was pathetic, I didn't care. Being close to her was all I wanted, and as she lay in my arms, I wasn't in any hurry to leave her side.

"Good morning," Nova mumbled against my chest, her breath tickling my skin.

"How'd you know I was awake?" I asked.

"Your breathing is getting heavier." She paused, tilting her head to look up at me. "So, either you're thinking hard or getting hard."

I laughed out loud as she raised her eyebrows. "Might be both with you naked and wrapped around me."

She smiled, snuggling closer against me. "Thank you for staying."

"Did you think I wouldn't?"

"Maybe. I thought you might have snuck out so your nan wouldn't know you'd been out all night."

"Judging by the message she sent you, I'm pretty sure she knew I wasn't coming back."

"Oh my God," she groaned, looking up at me again. "It's going to be so cringey when we go back in there and see her."

"Well..." I ran my hand down her arm, entwining my fingers with hers. "We can always combat that by staying here in bed all day."

"Hmm," she said, placing a soft kiss on my chest. "I might be on board with that idea, but... we'll still have to face her some time. And it will still be cringey. I mean, I used to just be Nova, her friendly neighbour. Now, I'm Nova, the woman who banged her grandson."

Laughing again, I let go of her hand and stroked the soft skin on her back. She let out a tiny sigh of pleasure. "So, what *do* you want to do today?"

"I hadn't really thought. Although... I was kind of wondering if you need to do anything for your blog. There are a few places around we could go and see. You could rack up a fair amount of content just in one day without going too far."

How was it possible that she kept getting better? Admittedly, I wasn't sure how much I could find of interest nearby in one day, but the fact she was interested enough in my work to ask if I needed more content was sweet. Sometimes, even I found what I did for a living a bit ridiculous, but she had never once mocked me. She'd just accepted it and looked me up, and now she wanted to help.

"Where did you have in mind?" I asked her. Now my ankle was fully healed, I could drive again, and I was looking forward to going further than the town for a change.

"I have a few ideas." She smiled. "What does a day of travel blogging involve for you?"

"More than you probably think," I told her honestly. Yes, I was a guy with a camera and internet access, but when it came down to it, there was a lot of photo and video editing involved, as well as writing in an appealing and informative way. I spent more time editing videos than almost anything else, but it was worth it. However, the amount of hours that stuff took was the main reason I had scheduled some things to post on most of my channels before I arrived in Devon. The post I'd made about being in Devon had thrown things off a little and had led to me hitting pause on my other posts. So, I needed to either make more local and current content, or let the other posts go out. There was nothing on my channels about any part of the UK, which, when I thought about it, was a bit ridiculous with me being English and all. If I did get some new content, it would mean having to spend the best part of a day getting it all ready to publish, but it was better than leaving everything to get stagnant for another couple of weeks.

WITHIN A COUPLE OF HOURS, AFTER I'D GONE BACK TO MY NAN'S TO GET showered and changed, Nova and I were standing in front of

Teignmouth Pier, wrapped up in our thick coats, shivering as the sea breeze whipped around us.

"Here?" I asked. "Really?"

I'd come armed with my phone, which was how I filmed most of my content, but also my camera, slung over my shoulder in its bag, just in case there was anything I needed to capture. My phone also took exceptional photos, but I liked the ability to change the settings depending on what I was trying to accomplish with each shot.

I didn't really mean what I was saying about being at the pier, I was just teasing her but she hadn't realised yet.

Nova blinked rapidly at my lack of enthusiasm. "Are you kidding? Please, please tell me you haven't forgotten how much fun you can have on a pier."

I shrugged. "All those claw machine things encouraging you to keep putting money in to win a soft toy. If you really want one, I could just buy you one."

She shook her head. "Your inability to enjoy the journey is rather ironic, considering what you do for a living." Nova took my hand and pulled me towards the doors. "Honestly, sometimes I think you've come so far, and then you say something like that. Besides, you cannot call yourself a photographer if you can't see the beauty in this structure!"

I laughed, holding my free hand up in surrender. "I see it, I see it! I was just screwing with you, I swear."

She rolled her eyes, and I let her drag me through the doors to be confronted by an array of games and machines flashing lights and playing music. It was an overwhelming cacophony of things, but the second my feet were inside, I understood exactly what she had been talking about. Being there reminded me of summers spent in Cornwall, in their amusement arcades. There always seemed to be a strange metallic scent in them, presumably the aroma of years' worth of coins dropping in and out of slots hanging in the air. It stirred another part of my inner child.

"We're going to need some change," I said, pulling my wallet from my coat pocket.

Nova grinned, and we headed over to the nearest change machine.

As we walked around, I took some photos of the interior, making sure not to get any people in my shots. I focused on the games, especially the more retro ones. It was unfortunate that we weren't able to go out onto the outside part of the pier that day, but there was plenty to do inside. Nova and I had a few games of air hockey, in which I kicked her ass. Then we played on the 2p push machines for a while and managed to bag ourselves a packet of sweets and a keyring in the shape of an ice cream. Finally, we played on one of the claw machines because Nova had taken a liking to some large light brown teddy bears holding big pink flowers that were inside it. However, after about ten quid, we gave up and walked away empty-handed.

It was fun to play around in there, and when we were finished, we took a slow walk back to the car. I took some photos of the sea on the way, appreciating the view as I had when we'd been at the top of Lea Mount.

Next up, we got back in the car and I drove us to Dartmoor using the built-in Satnav, which Nova had programmed a postcode into. She had directed me to a little village named Widecombe-in-the-Moor. It was so picturesque with lush greenery, small, unique shops and cafes, and a stunning church. I took my time with my camera. Nova happily waited for me as I perfected my shots. When I was done, she led me to one of the local pubs, The Rugglestone Inn. It was the perfect village pub, with a cosy vibe and amazing food.

Once we were done with lunch, we headed to Brixham, where we explored the shops. Nova managed to get some more of her Christmas shopping, and we wandered down to the harbour before finally heading back to Dawlish.

It had been an incredible day. When I'd been to Devon as a child, I hadn't seen any of the places Nova had shown me. I hadn't even heard of Brixham, and definitely not the quaint villages of Dartmoor. It was eye-opening how much there was to see in that part of England, and Nova was excited to have shared some of those things with me.

As we sat in the car outside her house, I noticed Nova watching me.

"So... life in Devon isn't so bad after all," I said, because I knew she knew what I was thinking. She'd witnessed my enthusiasm about the places we'd been to, and I didn't mind admitting I was wrong about there being little to do locally.

She grinned. "Does that mean I win?"

"Nope. Because I haven't fallen back in love with Christmas yet!"

"I have a photo of you in a reindeer apron that says otherwise."

"I was forced into wearing it and you can't pretend that's not true."

"Please," she scoffed. "You didn't once say no!"

Smiling, I placed my hand on her thigh. "Even so, I am not all the way sold on festive fun yet."

"Then I will have to work harder!"

She turned towards me as much as was possible in the confines of the car, resting her hand on mine. "Thank you," she said. "For letting me take the lead and show you around. I'm glad you had a nice time."

Smiling, I said, "I did. And now I have some content for the blog and my other channels."

Nova laughed. "I can't believe I made my TikTok debut today."

I'd got a bit of footage while we were on Teignmouth Pier of Nova and me taking turns on the claw machines. We were unsuccessful, but it was just something quirky and silly to show people. I didn't post it until we were in the car on the way home, but it had already had a few thousand hits and some comments. Lots of them wondering who the mysterious lady was in my video. I only hit like, refusing to give anything more away.

"You may be in more of my stuff when I go through it all," I told her. "I will spend some of tomorrow sorting through the videos and photos and editing them into something usable. You want to join me and see a day in the life of a blogger?"

"Yeah, but I have plans in the morning to do some more last-minute shopping with Mum. I will be free after one, though."

"Okay. In that case, I will go somewhere with Nan tomorrow morning. Maybe have lunch with her, and you can come over in the afternoon."

She smiled. "Sounds like a plan."

I leaned forward, my lips caressing hers. "I don't want to leave you."

Nova chuckled. "Me neither, but I think your nan will send out a search party if you don't go home soon."

"I doubt it, but I guess I should go in."

Nova nodded. "Yeah. I suppose so."

She kissed me once more, and then we reluctantly pulled apart and got out of the car. Nova paused to grab the things she'd bought from the backseat, and then I locked the car and she joined me on the path.

I stood looking at her for a moment, seeing the little wisps of hair that had fallen out of her ponytail as the day had gone on. She looked a little tired, which wasn't surprising since we'd been walking around for most of the day, but her eyes were still so bright, and she was still so freaking beautiful.

I reached out, resting my hand on her cheek. "Have a good evening, *dolcezza*."

The word came out of my mouth so naturally it surprised me, and still in a perfect Italian accent, as if I'd never stopped speaking the language.

When I first left Italy, I'd been speaking Italian fluently for close to six years. I'd had to pick it up quickly, and I did. But when I went to Australia, I had to switch back to using English, and there were times when Italian words came out randomly. It had been a long while since that had happened, though. And I'd never used that particular word with a woman before.

Nova's eyes sparkled, a flash of heat to them. "What does that mean?"

I smiled. "It means 'sweetness'. I'm not sure where that came from, although it's definitely fitting."

Her grin widened. "Please speak to me in Italian more often."

Laughing, I pressed my lips to hers. "Ci vediamo domani, bella signora," I whispered, and she let out a soft sigh.

"Honestly, I don't care if you just told me to wash your dirty socks." She wound her free arm around my neck, her eyes smouldering. "Everything sounds sexy in Italian."

She brushed a kiss on my lips, making it even harder to want to walk away from her.

"If it gets this reaction, I'll only speak in Italian." I felt her smile against my lips.

"That's okay with me."

CHAPTER 15

NOVA

Mum and I wandered into Presents of Dawlish, a gift shop that had been in town for as long as I could remember, and always a great place to browse. They had the most amazing selection of gifts, cards, and chocolates anyone could ever need. We were looking for a small additional gift for June. I had a photo on my phone of June and Trevor that I'd taken of them one afternoon when we were sitting in their garden back in early spring, and Mum had got the picture engraved onto a heart-shaped pendant that hung on a silver chain. We both knew the necklace would be more than enough for her, but we wanted to get her something extra too.

"I need to get something for Donovan," Mum said as we headed past the first section of the shop towards the back, where the cards were. "Have you got any ideas what he might like?"

The mention of his name sent the butterflies flapping around my stomach again, and my cheeks were heating. Thankfully, she was too busy browsing to notice. I hadn't told her about my last few days with him yet because I hadn't been sure how to bring it up.

"I don't know," I said. "Maybe beer. He likes a Peroni."

"Seems a bit impersonal. Can you think of anything else?"

"Honestly, he doesn't want anything. Because he's always

travelling, he doesn't really have a need for stuff. Beer and chocolate might be the best things."

We moved around to the side of the shop that homed chocolate gifts, and after searching for a bit, we decided to make the gift fun and got Donovan a chocolate reindeer.

"How has June been the last few days?" Mum asked as we continued to look around the shop, away from the chocolates and around to the glass cabinets containing a huge array of ornaments.

"Actually, she had a bit of a breakdown the day you asked if she and Donovan wanted to come for Christmas. Before you asked, obviously. The offer cheered her up, though."

"Poor thing," Mum said, tucking her hair behind her ear as she peered at some football merchandise in one of the display cases.

"Yeah. I went over that afternoon and we baked cookies. It was fun."

"Have you seen much of Donovan this week?"

Every single bit of him.

I kept the thought to myself, but something in my expression must have given me away.

"Nova?" Mum asked, in the way mums have that leaves no room for avoidance or arguments.

Heat radiated from my face, and I tried not to look directly at her, but I could sense her gaze on me. "Oh, God. Yes, I have seen a lot of him. We've been... doing stuff together."

Mum's eyes widened before she let out a small giggle of delight. "I knew it! I knew you liked him!"

"Please, stop," I said, walking down a little further to look at another display. "It's not... I mean... yes, I like him, but... it's nothing."

"Nova Louise McKay, don't give me that. I'm your mother, and I know when you like someone!" She was still laughing as she followed me. "This is great!"

I couldn't help giving in to a laugh too. She was so excited, and if I was honest with myself, I was too. I'd been trying so hard not to get swept up in this thing with him, but we had spent all evening and well into the early hours texting, even though he was only one house away.

If we'd had our way, he would have spent another night with me, but I told him to stay with June. It wasn't fair for me to take him away again, and I'd already been with him for the whole day. He was there to visit her, not me. The idea of seeing him that afternoon had my stomach in knots of excitement, though. I couldn't wait.

"How about this for June?" I asked, pointing to a small robin ornament and trying to distract her from the previous conversation. "She loves robins, and it would fit in well with the other ornaments she has in her cabinet in the hallway."

Mum peeked closer at it. "That's an idea. Also a lovely symbol of the season. Let me go and find someone to help us, but don't think you can change the subject so easily."

I rolled my eyes as she walked away. She was still grinning as she left, and I rubbed my hand over my tired eyes. She was going to be unbearable for the rest of the morning now, and I was going to have to deal with the little balloon of mixed happiness and fear swelling up and down in my stomach while she forced me to talk about Donovan.

I'd had the best day with him yesterday. It was fun to see him in work mode. I got to witness how focused he became when trying to capture the perfect photo. When he was looking around for information about what he was photographing, and taking little snippets into his mind, occasionally whipping out a notebook from his camera bag so he didn't forget. I wasn't sure if this was the process for all travel bloggers, but seeing him taking what he did so seriously was fascinating to me. It was also incredibly sexy, the way his eyes flitted around to take everything in, and how they lit up when he saw something that interested him. In between all of that, he continued to reach for my hand whenever his camera wasn't in his, and I got to learn more and more about the things he liked. Turned out, he was as obsessed with being near the sea as often as he could as I was, though he preferred warmer climes. He'd also loved Brixham harbour and talked about one day owning his own boat. As much as he liked the sea, he hated seafood, just like me, and it was strange how many things we found we had in common the more we talked.

I pulled out my phone, getting a pull to message him; not that we hadn't already messaged that morning. He had taken to texting me to say good morning, and it made me grin like an idiot.

You are so screwed.

I pushed the annoying thought aside, repeating my mantra to live in the moment as I looked at my phone and found there was already a message from him there.

> **Donovan**
> I'm taking Nan to Newton Abbot this morning, but I'll be back by 12 as she has lunch plans with a friend, so just come over when you're ready, dolcezza. xx

He added a winky face to the end of the message, and my stomach flipped again, remembering how he'd sounded when he'd said that word to me the day before.

I typed back:

> Okay. I will be there as soon as I can. Do you want me to bring something over for lunch? xx

> **Donovan**
> Gay's Creamery chicken and veg pie, please. We'll figure something out for dessert. xx

He added another winky face, making my insides squirm with need. It was a good thing he was going out because I was strongly considering abandoning my mother and going back to June's to jump on him.

I replied:

> Can't wait to see you!! xx

> **Donovan**
> Me too xxxx

I noted the extra kisses and smiled, looking forward to real ones later.

Mum returned with a member of staff, and we got June's gift and paid for it before heading out of the shop and back into the cold December day.

"So," Mum said, linking her arm through mine. "I want to hear all about what you've been getting up to with Donovan."

"No, you don't," I said, but there was no way to stop the rush of heat to my cheeks.

"Ohhh!" Mum said, laughing out loud. "So, this is moving fast!"

"Stop it," I told her, my cheeks now burning as she cackled beside me. It was lucky we were close, and she was the kind of mother I didn't mind sharing things with. Luckily for me, she wasn't the kind that would berate me for sleeping with him so soon. Perhaps she might have thought differently if it was anyone else, but she had been romanticising Donovan's return since she found out about it. Admittedly, two childhood friends reuniting and getting together did make for a cute tale, but we weren't heading that way. Not long-term, anyway. The reminder caused a sharp stab somewhere inside me, threatening to dampen my enjoyment of the now.

I had never been a dive in feet-first kind of girl when it came to relationships. I would tread fairly carefully until I was sure something had clicked. Everything was backwards with Donovan. We'd already had sex, yet I was still trying to learn who he was. It was supposed to be the other way around, but every time I looked at him and saw his exceptional smile and twinkling eyes, I forgot everything else. I couldn't keep a firm grip on my feelings because, with each day, they grew a little more. What was throwing my thoughts into chaos was the fact that I was pretty sure he felt the same way. Every time we saw each other, whether it had been a day or an hour, we were drawn together as if we had been apart for months. The way he kissed me. The way he touched me. His words. All of it seemed like more than just some fleeting thing. He was seeing the beauty in where we were, and although I hadn't got him hooked on Christmas again yet, I could see that changing too.

"Nova," Mum said, her tone less teasing and more understanding. "Talk to me, sweetheart."

As we weaved through locals doing their shopping, I sighed. "It's... something. Maybe. I like him a lot." Just saying the words made me ache a little with the need to be with him.

"And where does he stand?"

I shrugged. "I think maybe the same as me. I'm trying not to stress over it too much as he will be leaving sometime between now and mid-January." The idea made me feel a bit sick, but it was what it was. I thought again about June, and what she'd said about grabbing hold of moments where I could. What we had right then was enough. It had to be.

Mum smiled as if she understood exactly what I felt. "Do you think he might change his mind about leaving?"

"No. I don't think so. Yesterday, we went out together, and I saw just how much he loves what he does. I don't think anything will keep him here or in any one place for long. Maybe one day, but not yet. This is how it's always been, though, isn't it? I have him for a while, and then he leaves."

"Well, yes, but this is a bit different than when you were little."

I shook my head. "It's not really. He's here, and then he goes away. The only thing different now is it might be more than a year until I see him again."

The one thing I was relatively sure about was that he would come back to visit more now he'd got close to June again, but I wasn't counting on those visits being yearly. I supposed there was the chance we really *would* go back to exactly how things were before. We would see each other every Christmas, but at least this time we could stay in touch more easily.

Mum and I slowed our pace as we waited to cross the road and then cut through to The Lawn so we could head over to Brunswick Place, where there were a few more gift shops. As we walked, Mum said, "You said you spoke to Louise and Sam, and they will be coming over at Easter. Maybe he'll come back then."

"Maybe, but he didn't say so."

I hadn't thought about that before, but surely, if he'd planned to be here in a few months, he would have mentioned it. Of course, we hadn't kissed then. Things had sped up a hell of a lot since then.

"I have no idea how all of this is going to play out, Mum. But for now, I just want to make the most of it. If nothing else, at least we'll get to spend the whole of Christmas together instead of sneaking out to show each other our presents over the garden fence."

Laughing, Mum said, "The two of you were so cute, and such good friends back then. Whatever is meant to be will find its way, sweetheart."

My mum's wise words echoed in my head for the rest of the morning. Donovan and I had found our way back to each other once. Was it so crazy to think there was a reason for that? I might not have been a believer in fate, but I did believe there were lessons in everything I experienced, even if it wasn't always clear what they were. Until the lesson appeared, I intended to fly by the seat of my pants and see where I ended up.

I knocked on June's door just before one p.m., a bag containing two chicken and vegetable pies in my hand. Donovan dragged me inside by my wrist, closing the door and pushing me up against it with such speed I lost my breath.

"Hi," he said with a bright smile.

I'd barely managed to respond when his lips descended on mine hungrily, causing me to hit him in the back with the pies as my arms wrapped around him.

Warmth was breathed into me as his lips kissed mine with what was a now well-practised rhythm, and I pressed my hips into his, smiling at his very obvious happiness to see me.

"That was the longest nineteen hours ever," he mumbled into my neck, his lips nuzzling my skin.

"You counted?" I asked, chuckling as I tipped my head back a little, allowing him better access.

"I did." He lifted his head to look at me. "I would really like to keep doing this, but I'm not sure how much longer Nan will be, and I don't think she'll be too pleased if she can't get in because I'm doing you against the door."

His words caused a rush of heat through me, and I laughed, kissing him once more before reluctantly dropping my arms from around him. "Maybe you can do me against my front door later."

He groaned as he took my hand and led me to the kitchen, adjusting his jeans with his free hand. "I might hold you to that."

Set up at June's kitchen table was an open laptop with a photo of Teignmouth beach inside a photo editing program, his camera, his phone, and a ring light, which I assumed he'd used to shoot a video before I arrived. I cast my eyes over the equipment, amused he owned a ring light; something I associated with teenage girls using TikTok. Donovan didn't strike me as a guy who worried too much about being seen in the best light—in any aspect of the words—and he smirked as he saw me looking at it.

"Even bloggers want to look good on camera," he said. "Don't take the piss."

Looking up at him, I said, "I didn't say a word. It's very.... professional." My lips twitched and he rolled his eyes, even though he was still smiling.

"Give me the pie. I'm starving."

Within a few minutes, we'd cleared some space at the table to eat, chatting about our mornings as we polished off the food. Once we were finished and washed up, I made us both a cup of tea and then sat beside Donovan while he worked on his photo edit.

Watching him work, it was clear he was a perfectionist, and he cleaned up any flaws, anything that had snuck into the shot that could ruin it, undoing and redoing it until he was satisfied.

I'd kind of assumed blogging would be easy. Go to a place, take a photo or video, edit it if needed, write something, then post it. That itself took time, but it went way deeper for Donovan. He had TikTok, Instagram, a Facebook page, and a YouTube channel to manage too, as well as an actual website where his blog was. He'd put roughly twenty minutes of touching up just into one photo, let alone all the other things he had to do.

Once he was done with that, he saved the file. His folders were organised with a neatness that blew my mind. Each folder was labelled by year, then inside those, by month, and inside the month folders, by location.

"That is some high-level filing system you have there," I said, staring at his screen.

"I know, but I hate having to look too hard for a particular shot or album." He clicked out of the folder and turned to me. "I never expected to have a file with photos of England inside."

"Why not?" I asked, genuinely curious. "You talk about travelling the world, but England is a part of that."

Donovan nodded. "Yeah. It is. But I guess I thought because I spent some of my childhood here, it didn't count as 'travel'. It's the same reason I have nothing about Italy on my blog either. Even though I've been there a few times over the years to see my parents, I never write about it."

"Because it feels too familiar to you, or because it feels too personal?"

He paused for a moment as if thinking it over. "Both. I try hard not to let too much of me—the important, personal parts—get into the blog. Italy is where my mum and dad are, and I kind of like that nobody knows I grew up there. People know I am English, obviously, but up until I came back, I'd never said exactly where I was from."

"What made you share it now? You said the post you wrote about Dawlish was more personal than you usually get."

Another pause before he met my eye as he considered the question. "Honestly, I don't know. But if I hadn't, then you wouldn't have written the list, and we probably wouldn't be sitting here right now."

"Hmm," I said, nodding. "That's a fair point."

And another point in favour of fate. Or maybe not fate, but something. If he hadn't told me what he did, I wouldn't have looked him up, and I wouldn't have seen the post that had led to the re-writing of his Christmas. But by that same thought process, I could keep going down the road of 'ifs' forever. Whatever it was, it had brought us here. To this moment.

"Do you know when you'll be leaving yet?" I asked the question as casually as I could manage, even though my gut clenched, awaiting his answer.

Donovan smirked. "Had enough of me already?"

Not even close.

Worryingly, I was beginning to think I would never be able to get enough of him.

Rolling my eyes, I teased, "Not yet. Give it a few days, though."

He leaned forward, placing a hand on my cheek. "I'm still not sure when I'm leaving," he said. "But it definitely won't be this side of Christmas, so let's not think about that for now."

Looking into his eyes, crinkled at the corners as he smiled at me, my heart leapt just a little. He was so freaking beautiful it was unfair. As my heart rate picked up, I was sure its beat was saying, *Don't leave, don't leave, don't leave.* But I blocked it out as Donovan's lips touched mine. I had to because what I wanted wasn't possible. The only thing possible was to soak up every second I had with him.

The moment was interrupted by the sound of a key in the front door. I smiled as Donovan dropped his head then looked back up at me. June walked into the kitchen and dropped her handbag down by the kitchen table.

She smiled when she saw Donovan and me sitting together, but it didn't quite reach her eyes. "Are you okay?" Donovan asked, turning away from me to look at her.

June rubbed a weary hand across her forehead as her eyes shifted to the living room. "I am. Just... with it getting closer to Christmas it's..." she trailed off with a sigh. "This time last year, Trevor and I were out together having lunch with friends, and now it's just me. It's lovely having you two here, but it's just... different now. Sometimes, when I come home, I still hope there was some mistake and he'll be sitting in his chair, reading the paper. This exact day last year, we'd had lunch with Annie and Reg, and when we got home, big child that he was,

Trevor was sitting on the floor next to the Christmas tree, trying to figure out what his presents were. He nearly broke his bloody hip struggling to get up off the floor." She gave a watery laugh at the memory, and I got up from my seat and crossed the room to her.

"I remember," I said, wrapping my arm around her. "You called me to come and give you a hand getting him up."

She chuckled, and I remembered him laughing his ass off as June had scolded him, calling him an old fool for getting down on the floor. The more he laughed, the harder it was for him to get to his feet, and I giggled at the memory.

"Some days, the good memories are harder than the bad ones," June said. "Knowing we can't make any more is hard. And just... it was so sudden. If he'd been ill or showed any signs something was wrong... not that it's better since the end result is still the same. But I would have had more time to say the things I wanted to say." She leaned against me, and I tightened my arm around her.

It was far from the first occasion she had expressed the need to tell her husband all the things she didn't get a chance to. Aside from what I could only assume was a constant agony at losing the most important person in her life, she lived with an unending need to express all she felt for him. While I had done all I could to help her through the grieving process, this was one thing nobody could change for her.

"What would you say to him?" I asked.

"Ooh, so many things, my darling." June rested her head on my shoulder. "So many things."

"Do you talk to him when you visit his grave?" Donovan asked.

June shook her head. "Sometimes I talk to him when I'm on my own in the house, but it's usually just telling him about my day. The things I really want to say are still left unsaid."

I glanced at Donovan, and for some reason, I sensed we had the same idea.

"Come and sit down," Donovan said to June, gesturing to the chair I'd vacated. I released my hold on June, and she sat down in the chair beside him as he fumbled around in his laptop bag that was on the floor and pulled out a pen and a pad of lined paper. He placed it in front of her. "Write him a letter. Write down everything you're thinking. Everything you want to say, and then maybe we could take it to the cemetery for him."

I watched as June's eyes misted over at the idea. "You're the writer, not me."

"Well, maybe I'll write one too," he said, and I saw the moment their gazes connected. I could only see June's eyes from my position, but they filled with a mix of pain, love, and understanding so strong my own eyes filled with tears.

"Deal," June said, her voice breaking a little.

Donovan placed his hand over June's, which rested on the table. I couldn't stay. This was their time to break through this last barrier that still held them both back. Not from each other, but their grief. June had been holding onto this overwhelming wave of love she couldn't express. Of words and emotions she wanted her husband to hear, even if she couldn't physically speak them directly to him. And Donovan had been suppressing some long held-in form of grief that wasn't just for Trevor, but for his other grandad. He had a lot inside him too that needed to spill out, and I couldn't be there for it. This was for them. To connect and release all the emotion that had circulated inside them for so long with no escape.

Donovan glanced over his shoulder at me as June picked up the pen, and I offered him a small smile, then nodded towards the door to let him know I was leaving.

"Call me later," I mouthed, and he nodded, his eyes burning into mine with a sincerity that made my breath catch.

"Thank you," he mouthed back, and then turned back to the table, taking a couple of pieces of paper from the notepad for himself before handing it back to June.

Without a word, I pulled my boots back on and headed to my house, hoping they would both be okay once their pent-up feelings came to the surface.

CHAPTER 16

DONOVAN

Nan sat tapping her pen against the notepad, and I picked up a pen and stared at my own blank page. This was my idea. The way I processed things. Almost everything except grief, as it turned out. I made lists, weighed up options, and expressed anger, or concern, or frustration by dumping the contents of my brain onto a piece of paper, but never grief.

I'd never wanted to deal with it, really. Not that anyone does, but left to fester, it becomes so much bigger. And grief is big enough anyway.

I cast my mind back to the memories I'd thought of before. Of visits to see Nan and Grandad in Manchester, and in Dawlish, and when they'd visited us in Cornwall and Italy. About the humour Grandad always brought. About his kindness.

And then I thought about me. Where I'd been. What I'd been doing, and all the things I could have done. *Should* have done.

And then there was my nan, sitting beside me, writing words down in her curly handwriting. She was lost. Lonely. She was perhaps still a little angry with me, and I couldn't blame her.

I'd been so fucking self-centered it was unreal. I'd seen her break down twice since I'd been visiting, and if it had happened twice in a few weeks, what had it been like before? At the beginning, when it was so fresh. After six months, it was still pretty fresh. Still so raw and heavy. I'd kept away from her and my parents because of guilt, and that admission wasn't new to me. I'd said it to Nova, and I'd known exactly what I was doing when I was doing it. But the truth was, I had never been any good at processing grief. Maybe that's something that happens when you experience it when you're young. One minute, you're having the time of your life, and the world is perfect and fun and safe. Then, in an instant, it's dark. Safety no longer exists and you realise everything you have around you isn't assured. People won't always be there, and you have to learn how to cope with a huge chunk of your heart torn out.

If that was how I'd felt about Grandad Cain, how the hell did Nan deal with Grandad Trevor being gone? I had never been oblivious to her pain, I just didn't want to deal with it. I could never experience the loss of him as intensely as she or my mum did because I chose not to be close to him or to Nan. By leaving Italy as young as I did, I'd also put a divide between me and my parents. It was a bit different with them because I stayed in touch with them, but there was some warped logic in my mind that if I got used to not being around them, it would be easier when they passed. It didn't matter that I knew that wouldn't truly be the case, but I was happy to con myself for as long as I could.

It seemed, though, the con was over now.

As if a switch had been flicked, words finally began to pour out on the page.

Grandad,
I've been thinking a lot lately. Since I came to see Nan. Well, I tried not to think at first, but I've been forced to take a look at the last few years from a different point of view.
I travelled, Grandad. All over the world. Saw things I never thought I'd see and met people I never thought I'd get along with. People with amazing stories that have changed the way I looked at things.

I made some mistakes. Big ones. The biggest being that seeking the next adventure meant I didn't have to focus on what was actually important.

And then you were gone.

I hate ever admitting I was wrong, but I was. I was wrong to not call you more, and to not reply to your emails. Even worse, I was wrong for not coming back until it was too late. I could have known you better. Listened to stories you had to tell about your life like I listened to all those strangers on my travels.

That's the real tragedy of it. I knew strangers better than I knew you and Nan. And you know what's even worse? I didn't want to come here for Christmas. Not because I have no feelings, but because I didn't want to face Nan. To see how disappointed she was that I wasn't here for your funeral.

I made it all about me.

And as if all that wasn't enough, I just assumed Nan would be okay here on her own. She's tough. Always has been. As it turned out, a lot of her strength was tied to you. She could face anything with you at her side, and now, her other half is missing.

If you were still here, I would tell you how sorry I am. For not seeing you more, and for not talking to you more. It's my loss because now I will never know you the way I should have. I left it too late.

I'm sorry for not coming to your funeral.

It's not that I didn't care. I always cared. Time, as it so often seems to do, made a fool of me. It passed so fast. Ten years gone in a flash.

I did love you, and I love Nan. And I'm so, so sorry for not being a better grandson. You both deserved more from me, *and I swear with everything I have I will do better from now on.*

I hope you can forgive me as I'm not sure I'll be able to fully forgive myself.

Love always,

Donovan

A small splash hit the bottom of the piece of paper, and I wiped it away, then brushed away the drops of moisture that sat unshed in my eyes. I blew out a slow breath, reading over my words again. With each one, a heavy knot grew in my chest until it ached so badly my whole body grew rigid.

Just the way Nan had in the cafe.

Why did it hurt so much now? Why did it feel like my fucking heart was about to explode in a shower of anger and anguish and regret?

"Let it go, my darling."

Nan's words were all it took for a sob, deep and long, to pour from my lips. I pushed my letter aside and curled forward, my head resting on my arm as tears began to soak my sleeve.

Nan shuffled her chair closer to mine and wound her arm around my back, and I could hear her crying too as she tried to comfort me.

"I'm sorry," I said. "I'm sorry."

Her hand gently rubbed my back. "It's all right, sweetheart. It's all right."

It wasn't. I knew she forgave me, but in that moment, all I wanted was to go back in time and do things right. Better. To be someone who deserved to grieve. The harsh reality was that I didn't. How could I grieve someone I hardly knew?

"Your grandad always said you would come back when you were ready, and you did."

"Too late," I said. "Way too late."

"For him, perhaps. And that is something we can't change. But you did come back. You're here. You might think it was for the wrong reasons, but whatever they were, you still came. You could have stayed away forever."

Lifting my head slowly, I wiped my eyes, and Nan shifted over a bit so I could straighten up. "I missed out, Nan. On knowing Grandad."

She nodded. "Yes. But I don't think that is a mistake you're going to make again."

For some reason, I had the strangest idea she wasn't just talking about herself, and I raised an eyebrow.

Nan smiled. "You do what you need to do, Donovan, but don't try to pretend you don't have feelings for the girl next door. She's special. And if you break her heart, I'll break your legs."

I snorted out a laugh, but my nan would stay true to her word.

Which didn't help me with the email currently tormenting me in my inbox I knew I should tell both of them about.

"Have you finished your letter yet?" I asked, wiping my eyes again and hoping to change the subject.

"Nearly," Nan replied, turning back to her piece of paper. "I think I'll only need a few minutes. Once I'm done, we can take our letters to the cemetery like you said, and then I want you to go and see Nova again. Take her out for a drink or something."

I smiled, wanting nothing more than to do those things. But the high level of emotion of the day made me want to stay with Nan too. I couldn't leave her completely alone while she was emotional, even if writing the letters had helped.

"I could ask her to come back here," I said. "Maybe we could get a takeaway tonight and watch some Christmas movies together."

Nan's grin told me she fully appreciated the offer. "We can do that, but if you two would rather be alone together, that's okay with me too. Don't hang around here on my account."

"But I'm here to see you," I pointed out.

"Yes, but it's also important that we're not tripping over each other all the time. I'd love to spend the evening with you both, but if you want to go out, don't feel like you *have* to be with me."

I didn't. Not anymore. At first, it had been a chore and a challenge.

Now, though, I appreciated the time with her. Being around her had triggered a need to be around my family more, and I couldn't wait to see my parents again either. I just wasn't sure when that might be now.

"Okay," I said, standing up. "You finish your letter, and I'll text Nova about tonight."

"Just tell her to come over as soon as we're back from the cemetery," Nan said with a laugh. "I know you've hardly seen her today."

"You're making me sound like a loser," I said, pulling my phone from my pocket, but I grinned as I spoke.

"Nothing wrong with wanting to be around someone you like." She said the words as she picked up her pen, and I didn't reply, unwilling to pull her focus any more since she wanted to get her letter finished. I hadn't meant to punctuate her own reflections with my breakdown, and I knew she still had things she wanted to say, so I went into the living room and sat down to text Nova.

Why did I miss her already? She'd been gone for such a short while. But like Nan said, I'd hardly seen her since she'd only arrived at lunchtime. That was all it was.

I ran a hand through my hair, then rubbed my eyes, heaving out a sigh. For someone who tried not to feel too much, the day had been emotional and draining. I would have liked to just be with Nova, even though she was a big part of the reason my feelings were all over the fucking place. But if I was honest, I loved Nova being in Nan's house with us. The friendship between them was strong and sweet. It seemed weird that two people so far apart in age would get along so well, but Nova had an element of old soul about her. It was something I seemed to possess also, in a way. As much as I loved the thrill of being out in the world, I also liked time to myself to think about what I'd experienced. In the last couple of weeks, I'd learned to also see the much bigger picture. To see *myself* and fix the things about me I hadn't liked when I'd looked deeper.

I wasn't sure I'd truly changed much, really, though. When it came down to it, there would probably always be a little part of me that was self-centred. That wanted my way and wouldn't budge. I'd allowed myself to open up and get to know my nan, and Nova was able to get under my skin like nobody else ever had, but that didn't mean I wouldn't somehow always find a way to put myself first.

"OH MY GOD," NOVA SAID, LEANING BACK AGAINST THE SOFA AFTER swallowing one final sweet and sour chicken ball. "I should have stopped eating about five minutes ago." She pulled at the waistband of her jeans for a moment, then rested a hand on her stomach.

Between us, Nova, Nan, and I had just eaten a Chinese banquet consisting of way more dishes than we ever should have ordered, but it was worth every single mouthful.

Nan put her lap tray containing her empty plate onto the floor by her feet and said, "I'm stuffed too. I won't need to eat for a week now!"

Nova laughed. "Don't let my mum hear you say that. Knowing her, she's got enough Christmas food to feed a small army."

"Amateurs," I said, grinning, even though I was also entirely too full. "We'll be nibbling at the rest of the leftovers within an hour, I bet you."

"Not me," Nan said. "I am full up."

Nova eyed the remaining sweet and sour balls before groaning. "Why does it have to taste so good? I've had more than enough, but I still want more."

"Will I have to carry you back to your house tonight?" I asked.

She looked up at me and nodded, eyes wide with glee at the idea of not having to walk. "Please."

"You're more than welcome to stay here tonight," Nan said, causing us both to spin our heads in her direction. She rolled her eyes. "I'm old, not stupid. You're both fully grown adults, and if you want to stay here, that's fine with me."

My eyes lit up at the prospect of Nova spending the night. "What do you think?" I asked her. "Wanna stay?"

She smiled. "Sure." She looked back at Nan. "Thank you."

"It's not a problem, my love." She gazed at us with a fondness in her eyes, like she was enjoying us all being together, and a stab of guilt plunged into my insides.

This wasn't going to last for too much longer. Us all being in the same place. I didn't mind admitting I liked the way we were all now so relaxed around each other, but I *dis*liked that it would be over soon. The tension between me and Nan was gone. Since we'd talked and figured out a way to let out some of our grief, it was better.

We'd stayed at the cemetery longer than most people usually would on a chilly day, but we set our letters down, tucked right away behind the flowers so nobody would easily see them and take our personal thoughts to do with as they pleased. The likelihood was, it would rain soon, and the ink would run so it would all be ineligible anyway. But doing that one thing together had made us closer. There was comfort in being around her now. One I hadn't even known I was missing.

And then there was Nova. Fuck. I didn't understand what the hell was happening to me when it came to her. I just knew since the first moment I kissed her, I wanted to be around her all the time. Wanted to touch her. And when I wasn't with her, the thing on my mind the most was when I could see her again.

Don't. You always knew the deal. You asked her to live in the moment with you, and you're *not even doing that.*

It was getting harder to, though. Maybe the days running out wasn't such a bad thing after all. The sooner I was gone and the further away I was, the easier it would be to stop thinking about her.

Even I knew that was a load of bollocks, but I wasn't above kidding myself to make a situation easier. It was kind of my thing. It was what had led to me unleashing years' worth of bottled-up agony earlier. I may have got a handle on dealing with grief, but I wasn't suddenly issue-free.

There was a suggestion of a movie on Netflix, and once it began, I pulled Nova onto my lap. She sat sideways facing the TV, her legs straightened out on the sofa as she snuggled into my chest. Through the whole movie, our fingers were entwined, and my thumb occasionally stroked across her knuckles as if I were reminding myself this was real. That she wasn't just some figment of my imagination. She was curled in against me like there was nowhere else she wanted to be, and I wanted the movie to stretch on so I didn't have to think about anything other than the sensation of her against me, her hand in mine.

My chest began to ache again, and it was a feeling that continued until we eventually found ourselves upstairs, in bed.

"You know, it was really polite of your nan not to mention that I didn't bring any pyjamas here, nor did I go home to get some," Nova said as she shuffled across the bed towards me wearing only her underwear—a matching lacy white bra and knickers set that made her look both innocent and sinful.

I chuckled as I wrapped my arms around her. "I guess she knew it was possible they wouldn't stay on for long."

"Is that true?" she asked, lifting her head to look at me. Her brown eyes were serious. "You've been quiet tonight."

I considered mentioning the obvious fact we had been watching movies, but we both knew that wasn't what she meant.

"I'm sorry," I told her, kissing her forehead. "It's just been a long day after all the stuff with Nan."

Liar.

It was only a partial lie. I felt better for getting so much out of my system earlier, but I also felt tired. Processing so many things had taken it out of me, but like the selfish prick I was, I still wanted Nova with me. Wanted to soak up as much of her as I could while I had the chance.

"I understand," she said with a soft smile. "Honestly, if all we do tonight is this, that's okay."

"Huh," I teased. "I guess the appeal of me has worn off already."

Nova shook her head. "Nope. Not at all. I just... I like being close to you in whatever way I can."

I closed my eyes at her words, wishing I'd kept my emotions shut off. It was a hell of a lot easier that way. Much simpler than the heavy weight that hung over me every time I thought about leaving. About my decisions.

I rested my head on top of hers, breathing in the apple scent of her shampoo.

"Dolcezza," I murmured. "Sei così perfetto. Vorrei poterti portare con me."

She wriggled closer. "What does that mean?"

"It means I want to take the rest of your clothes off."

More lies, but somehow, it was easier for me to say what I was thinking in Italian, so she didn't understand what it really meant. *You're so perfect. I wish I could take you with me.*

"I don't have a problem with that," Nova whispered, her lips finding my neck and kissing softly down and along my shoulder. I moved my hands up her back, unhooking her bra, then reached up to pull the straps down her arms.

Living in the moment had never been so incredible and so freaking conflicting. But I wasn't going to stop. I wanted her. Needed her.

And so, I lost myself in her again, all the while knowing this would come crashing down around us both sooner than either of us wanted.

CHAPTER 17

NOVA

WAKING UP BESIDE DONOVAN WAS FAST BECOMING A THING I LOVED. I couldn't get enough of being surrounded by him, his large frame enveloping me. If it hadn't been two days before Christmas, I would have considered asking if he wanted to take things back to mine and stay in bed there all day. But I had things I needed to do. Plus, we still had one thing to do on our list. It had been put on hold the last couple of days, but I wanted to complete it because I needed to see him in the elf costume he'd vowed to wear if I wore him down and made him love Christmas again.

Just as we had the day before, we'd gone our separate ways for the morning. I went home to wrap up the last of my gifts, ready to take them to my parents' house on Christmas morning. The days had flown by over the past few weeks. Thankfully, I was fairly well organised, and at least I didn't have to worry about cooking Christmas dinner for myself, so that was one less hassle for me.

The last thing left on the Christmas hit list was "Judge me". When Donovan and I were kids, we'd done a lot of craft stuff with his mum, and one of our activities had been to make a Christmas card, and Donovan's dad and grandad would judge them. We'd both won once, so technically, this was the tie-breaker round, and June had already agreed to be the judge. Donovan, however, didn't know what we were doing until he entered my living room and saw an array of craft supplies laid out across my coffee table. There was a pile of white A4 card, glue, various coloured pencils and felt tip pens, some coloured glitter glue pens, a range of Christmas-themed stickers, some Christmas stencils, and a bag full of mini pom-poms, pipe cleaners, and googly eyes.

"Bloody hell," he said with a laugh as he stared at the items on the table. "This brings back some memories."

"That's kind of the point." I poked my tongue out at him playfully.

"You're a big kid, you know that, don't you?" He wrapped his arms around me and pulled me close against him, my hands resting on his waist.

I might have taken the remark as a dig a week or so ago. Now, it simply made me grin. "And you are still too serious. So, this should be entertaining."

"You aren't expecting any masterpieces, are you?" he asked, then kissed me gently. "Because art is definitely not my strong point."

Laughing, I said, "Is this a good time to tell you that art is my main speciality and I'm the one who created many of the displays in the school classrooms?"

His eyes widened. "Oh, that's an unfair advantage you never used to have," he teased, holding his hands up. "I can't go into a competition with an expert when I'm just an amateur."

Releasing my hold on him, I dropped down to the floor by the coffee table. "I thought you liked a challenge." I said it knowing full well he also didn't like to lose. Even at something as silly as a Christmas card-making contest.

Donovan sat down at the other side of the table. "I do. But not one I know I *definitely* can't win."

"But you don't know," I pointed out. "June is going to decide the winner, and she might find your effort endearing."

The way he looked at me, eyes half-narrowed but still sparkling made me laugh out loud. "Bring it on!" he said, lifting a piece of card from the pile and pulling it towards him. "And don't be cheating by looking at what I'm doing," he added, pulling the bag of assorted craft bits and putting it between us so I could no longer see his project.

"Fine. I look forward to kicking your ass!"

We grinned at each other before getting to work.

I reached for a piece of card and then a gold glitter glue pen. I hadn't used one of those in years, and as I took the lid off it, the adhesive smell transported me back to my childhood, when every piece of 'artwork' I made involved glitter glue pens.

I began to very carefully write *merry* across the card in block letters, hoping the gold would last enough to colour the whole word in. Thankfully, it did, but there was no way it would last to write *Christmas*, so I put the lid back on and reached for the red pen.

I'd been so engrossed that I hadn't looked at Donovan for a while, but he seemed equally involved in his card. The concentration on his face was cute, and I giggled as I watched him. I couldn't see exactly what he was doing, but his tongue was out slightly as he focused. It looked like he was trying to peel off a sticker, but I realised his short nails wouldn't allow it.

"Need some help?" I asked, and he shook his head.

"I got it," he answered, and I saw him move his hands as if sticking something down.

It occurred to me as I started to write my second word on my card that I wouldn't be able to do much around the first word until the glue dried, and from memory, I recalled that took a long-ass time.

"Do you want a drink?" I asked, realising I should have asked when he arrived. Unfortunately, his arms around me had made me forget my manners.

He glanced up at me. "Yes, please. Do you still have hot chocolate and whipped cream?"

My lips twitched as his beautiful blues twinkled with mischief. "I always have whipped cream." My tone was seductive, my lower lip pouted out before I licked my tongue across it.

He let out a low groan. "I know what you're doing, lady, and you're not going to distract me with your dirty mouth."

His words and his gaze caused heat to blossom inside me, but I just gave a casual shrug as if I wasn't affected before walking to the kitchen, swaying my hips as I went.

"Tease," he muttered, making me laugh.

I headed for my Tassimo machine—which I was sure might have been considered cheating to make hot chocolate—and flicked the switch to turn it on before lifting the lid and popping in a pod. Once I'd pressed the button, glass mug ready underneath, I went to the fridge for the whipped cream. As I shook the can, my mind drifted to the fun Donovan and I could have with it, but I pushed the thought aside to revisit later.

The hissing of the machine as it steamed was noisy, and while I waited for it to calm down, I went to the cupboard in the corner of my kitchen where I kept all of my sweet treats to get the marshmallows. Once the first drink was done, I gave it a stir, then squirted out a generous helping of cream and topped it with pink and white marshmallows. I set the next mug up and put in a fresh pod, pressing the button and letting myself become mesmerised by the cream as it began to melt into the already-made drink. Once the other was ready, I picked them up and walked towards the kitchen door. As I did so, I heard a male voice in the room that wasn't Donovan's. Nobody had come in as I would have heard the doorbell, but there was definitely a voice coming from the living room. Also, the accent wasn't English. It sounded Australian from a distance.

I hadn't intended to listen; I was just trying to deliver the drinks, but my feet stopped in their tracks just as I heard the excited voice say, "Oh my God. I can't believe this is happening. I will see you at the end of next week in the fucking Maldives!"

My heart began to pound as a flood of emotions rushed through me. The high level of what-the-fuckery was drowning out most other thoughts I had. Donovan was grinning as he pressed something on his phone, but when he looked up and saw me, his smile dropped instantly.

I was still having trouble forming a solid thought, but my heart continued to hammer as I walked into the room and placed the drinks down on the tiny bit of available space left on the coffee table.

He kept his gaze on me as if weighing up whether to say anything. Possibly wondering if I'd heard what was said. I wasn't sure how my expression wasn't showing anything that made my thoughts clear. Perhaps my features had frozen as much as my feet had.

That, or I was trying to decide if I was more angry or upset.

Had he just planned his next trip while in my house, or worse, had he been planning this for a while without mentioning it?

Whether I was angry would highly depend on whether he'd been pretending he didn't know when he was leaving or if this had just happened in the past few hours. Unfortunately, I couldn't seem to get any words to leave my lips.

"You heard that, didn't you?" he asked.

All I could manage was a nod as a lump formed in my throat. I swallowed it down because, did I really have a right to be upset? If *I'd* concluded he would be staying until January, that was on me because he'd never confirmed it. That was a hope I'd carried. A belief I'd formed because of how close we'd become. And yet he'd very recently told me no plans had been made for his leaving, but the message I'd overheard sounded like a confirmation. A previously arranged thing.

Guilt seemed to fill his eyes.

Donovan got to his feet and took my hands in his. "Can we sit down, please?"

When I neither agreed nor declined, he pulled me to the sofa and we both sat down on the edge, knees pointed towards each other but not touching, our hands no longer joined.

"Obviously," he began, "you weren't supposed to hear that."

Then why play it out loud in my house? The words were there in my mind, but they still wouldn't come out of my mouth as annoyance and sadness continued to battle in my brain.

"Fuck, Nova," he said, blowing out a breath. "I'm so sorry. I didn't want you to find out like that."

"I'm not sure exactly what I've found out," I said, my voice sounding a little croaky due to the dryness in my throat, and I swallowed to moisten it. "What's going on?"

He inhaled deeply. Concern and guilt continued to swirl in his gaze, and he said, "That was a friend of mine. His name's Darren, and I met him on one of my first trips to Australia. He was backpacking like me, and we travelled together for a while. When I got with Paige, we went in different directions. He was in Europe for years, but we stayed in touch and he does the same thing for a living as me. His following isn't as big as mine, but it's big enough to make him well-known." He paused. "Last week, he was approached by the owners of a brand new resort in the Maldives after a friend of his put in a good word for him. They want him to spend four weeks at their resort, telling his followers what it's all about and also taking photos for their website, and they want to pay him for it all. Darren is confident in his blogging and filmography skills, but he's always been impressed with my photography, so he asked if there was any chance he and I could collaborate on the project. The resort has only been open for a month, and they want people who can help them get the word out. While they can afford the best of the best for everything in terms of marketing, the owners are looking for some social media clout, and we have that. With Darren alone, it would have been enough, but with me on board as well, they will be able to reach hundreds of thousands of travel-obsessed people alongside their more traditional promotional efforts. They offered us a deal that was impossible to refuse, and because of the collab, Darren and I stand to make a lot more money from our channels as a bonus."

His guilt was being replaced by excitement, his eyes lighting up the more he told me, and my stomach twinged. I couldn't pretend it didn't hurt a little that he was so eager to leave, but this was a huge opportunity for him. One any sane person would have difficulty refusing, so I just nodded my understanding, the lump re-forming in my throat.

Four weeks. He could always come back afterwards, right?

"Nova, this is huge," he said, taking my hand. "It's unusual for anything like this to come up, but the owners had spoken to some of their team, looking for influencers, and Darren had a connection with one of them. For anyone to offer something like this is almost unheard of. And there's also a chance for more work after. If they like what we do, they said they'd be interested in us going to the resort they're preparing in the Philippines that will be opening next summer, and maybe visiting some of the resorts they have that are already open from February to April. It wouldn't be constant through those months, but a few weeks here and there when they want it."

So, not four weeks. More like six months before he'd be done with the initial commitment to check out their resorts, and then on to the next one for a few weeks. I couldn't speak for his friend, but I'd seen what Donovan could do, and there was no doubt in my mind he would be hired for longer than a month.

"Donovan... when did this negotiation begin?" I asked, and he grimaced, letting go of my hand and leaning back slightly before he spoke.

"Darren reached out last week, but I didn't expect it to go any further than being an idea. I knew the job was his, but I didn't think they'd want to pay both of us, no matter how rich they are. They're a huge company, and they have a team of every kind of expert they could need without bothering with a couple of travel bloggers. Once they saw the influence we have, they decided they couldn't afford not to work with us. They want us to start working the first week of January and offered to pay for our flights out on December 28th, so we can spend some time settling in, meeting the bosses to find out the detailed plan of what they want, and then sorting it all out. I've had a few video calls with them over the last few days, but they want to meet us in person as soon as possible."

Five days. He's leaving in five days.

I raised my eyebrows. When did he have these meetings? Most of his time that week, he'd been with me. Was he having calls in between our dates? More importantly, if he'd told me a few days ago these talks were happening, would I have let myself get closer to him? Invited him into my bed?

I couldn't answer that. Maybe I would have done everything just the same anyway. But the problem for me was that he had been lying to me about when he was leaving, and it left a bad taste in my mouth.

More so because there had been no hint of him wavering as he uttered half-truths while looking into my eyes.

"Nova, talk to me. Please."

I wiped my palms on my jeans; they'd grown sweaty with tension while I'd been listening to him and processing his words. "Why didn't you tell me about this as soon as you knew it was a possibility? Before anything happened between us, you knew this was something that could happen. So, why not mention it?"

He lowered his head for a second before looking back up at me. "When it was just an idea, I didn't think I needed to mention it. And then, when talks began, I still didn't believe it would work out. Then everything moved quickly, and Darren and I agreed we needed to jump on this chance, but at the same time, I was getting closer to you. You asked Nan and me to spend Christmas with your parents, and I just... I didn't want to ruin the day with both of us thinking about how soon I'd be leaving."

"And how did you think I would feel when you dropped it on me after Christmas that you would be leaving in a couple of days with no prior warning?"

He rubbed his hands over his hair, regret pouring off him so tangibly it threatened to knock me backwards. "I know, okay? I know. I just thought it would be easier to-"

"What, Donovan? It was easier to pretend?" I stood up as my feelings began to clarify themselves. The sadness parted from the anger, and the latter was ready to let loose. "Were you even going to tell me, or was I just going to wake up one morning and find you gone?" When he didn't answer, I shook my head and turned away, pacing to the other side of the room. "You know what makes this so shitty? Yesterday, I asked you if you knew when you were leaving, and you looked me right in the fucking eye and said you didn't know. But you did, didn't you?"

Donovan nodded. "Yeah. I knew."

I dropped my head back, looking up at the ceiling as I heaved out a breath.

I'd been prepared for the moment he would tell me it was time for him to go. I always knew this... whatever it was between us wasn't forever. And it was always going to be painful when it ended. But the fact I'd trusted him to be honest with me about his plans hurt more than his leaving ever could have. I'd expected more from him after everything. After how much he'd begun to open up.

After the way he'd made love to me, making me feel like the two of us entwined together was the only thing that mattered.

Maybe none of it ever mattered to him. If he could look straight at me and lie, I guessed I wasn't worth the truth.

And that sucked when the truth was the only thing I'd ever expected from him.

As I opened my eyes, I found Donovan standing in front of me, and his stupid, pretty blue gaze was filled with apologies. I wanted to say something to him, I just didn't know what the words were. The only thing I knew was that my heart hurt, and the bubble I'd lived in for the last few days had popped, leaving me flailing instead of carrying me along in its gentle hold.

"Nova, I never wanted it to be like this," he said softly. "I just wanted things to stay the way they were for as long as possible." When I didn't respond, he said, "Did you really expect me to give up everything I've built for you?"

I didn't. Of course I didn't. I hadn't once believed he would, but the way he'd said 'for you' as if I were so unimportant to him hit me right in the gut, so much so that I couldn't look at him.

Shaking my head again, I said, "I thought, after the last few weeks, you'd know me better than that. Have I ever asked you to stay here?"

"No. I know you wouldn't. But that doesn't mean you weren't thinking it."

Finally looking up at him again, I saw a change in his expression. He was reverting right in front of my eyes. Like all the things he'd said to me were fake. The times he'd said he missed me, giving me a cute Italian nickname, texting me almost all night when we weren't together. The teasing. The bond we'd formed.

And those kisses. Nothing about them had felt phony, and yet suddenly, his eyes had stopped holding that fondness I was used to seeing. He was looking at me like I was just another random girl who wanted something from him. As much as I cared about him, I never wanted anything but his time for as long as he was here. Whether I'd thought about him staying was irrelevant. I'd never pushed it onto him because it was my thing to deal with.

"Don't look at me like that," he said, turning away from me like I was the one who was suddenly different. I had no clue what my expression portrayed; I could only assume it was confused as hell because that about summed it up. "You can't get angry about me taking a job."

"I'm angry you lied about it, Donovan!"

"But I told you why!" He spun around to look at me again. "I didn't want to ruin the time we had left!"

"Well, it's ruined now! If you'd just been honest about it-"

"Oh, you wouldn't have been bothered? You think we would have had a lovely Christmas with both of us thinking about me getting on a plane in a few days?" He threw his hands in the air, letting them thud back down against his sides as he turned away from me again.

"We would have done the same as we have been!"

"You think it would have been that easy to pretend things were normal?"

"Well, *you've* managed just fine for the last few days!"

The words flew out before I could stop them, and it was a cheap, unfair shot, but there was truth at the heart of it. He *had* been pretending. He had outright lied to me, and even if he thought he was doing it for the right reasons, that didn't make it okay.

"You know, what? Fuck this." He turned to me, walking back to me until we were face to face. His eyes were stormy, his jaw tight, and his whole posture rigid. "All of this, it was you who did it. You were the one who pushed for us to be around each other." He gestured towards the coffee table, where our half-finished cards lay, now forgotten. "Why did you do this? You must have spent a fucking fortune on all this stuff. Food, movies, baking and craft supplies. Why?"

"Why?" I asked, taking a step closer to him. "Because when I found out who you were, it didn't make any sense that you could be such a different person than the one I used to know, and I just wanted you to feel *something*. To show me there was a human in there somewhere because you were so cold when you arrived. You resented that you had to come and be with June. I wanted you to care about something other than yourself. To remember what it's like to let go and have fun!"

"Newsflash, Nova. We're not kids anymore. Life isn't always fun." The scorn poured from his words, and with each one, I wished I'd stayed away from him.

Who the hell was he? Ten minutes before, we'd been making innuendos about whipped cream, and now we were back to being almost strangers again. How did he just switch off his emotions like that? We were both shouting, but he was looking through me now.

"You need to go," I said quietly.

For the briefest of moments, the Donovan I'd been getting to know reappeared, his eyes softening and his shoulders sagging. It took all of my strength not to throw myself into his arms, but just like that, his walls were back up, and he nodded before turning and walking out.

CHAPTER 18

DONOVAN

You fucking idiot. You absolute fucking dick.

The words tormented me as I left Nova's house and headed straight for my car. I didn't know where the hell I was going, but I just needed to get away. Off that street and anywhere but near the place I had messed up so spectacularly. I'd stared at her, listening to her perfectly valid frustrations, and all I could think to do was back the hell off. Talk to her as if she was being unreasonable and I'd done nothing wrong.

I lied to her. I sat with her in my nan's kitchen a day ago and told her I had no idea when I was leaving, though, even as I said it, the flights were being booked for the 28th.

I turned out of Nan's street along John Nash Drive. Dawlish was not designed for the speed I wanted to drive. I wanted to get out onto an open road and floor it, trying to outrun my thoughts because I hadn't been fair to Nova. Didn't matter how I tried to excuse it.

When this new opportunity had come up, my reasons for not telling her had nothing to do with whether I thought she deserved to know. It was just that I honestly didn't think it would come to fruition. As a travel blogger, people offered opportunities all the time. Sometimes I didn't want them. Sometimes I did, and then they fell through. This one was so fucking exciting to me I couldn't let myself think about it until it was all official. But by then, Nova and I had kissed, and telling her the truth would have made Christmas harder, even if she thought it wouldn't. It would have been solemn—more than it would have been anyway with Nan grieving. I just wanted to let Nova enjoy it. Wanted to carry the weight of my leaving on my own. It was fucking heavy, but I hadn't wanted to put it on her.

I also knew telling her after Christmas would make her hate me for keeping it to myself, but it was a risk I was prepared to take to not ruin the season she loved the most.

Turning down Oak Hill, I huffed out a long breath as my stomach began to twist.

If she hated me, leaving would be easier.

My vision blurred for a second, and I blinked to clear it, and then focused harder on the road so I didn't cause an accident due to my self-indulgent self-pity.

Nothing in my life had ever caused me more conflicting thoughts.

I wanted this job, and the deal was sealed. I was going. The idea of being out in the world again made my veins buzz with anticipation, especially at a resort as impressive as the one in the Maldives. I could practically taste the rum just thinking about the place. The sunshine. The beaches. A stunning apartment to live in with one of my oldest travel friends. Maybe it was wrong, but I hadn't had a second of hesitation about taking this project on.

But that didn't mean I didn't think about Nova. About leaving her and Nan behind sooner than I had intended to.

Both of them had given me a lot to think about. Nan and I had buried any remaining animosity that lingered between us, but Nova was something different altogether.

She'd made being in Devon better. I was sure just being with Nan would have become easier eventually anyway, and we would have gone to some places I hadn't seen before, and I would have fully appreciated what a great county it was. But Nova had made the whole experience fun. She'd seen me in a way that scared me, yet I didn't mind because she never pushed for more than I wanted to give.

My insinuation that she had done just that only proved what a total twat I was, but it was too late to take it back now.

Once I'd made it to town, I parked in a space in Brunswick Place, and after putting a ticket on my car, I headed for the seafront.

The air was frigid, and I'd only brought my light denim jacket with me because I hadn't planned to walk further than Nova's house from my nan's. I buttoned it up as I walked, and then stuffed my hands in my pockets, keeping my head down until I reached the viaduct and stepped onto the sea wall.

Even though it was cold, the winter sun was shining, making the waves glisten. I slowed my pace as I walked along the wall towards Coryton Cove. The smell of the salty sea air calmed me a little, and I breathed in deeply, a million memories of beach days flooding my mind. Grandad Cain took me to the beach even in winter, and we would always have fish and chips afterwards. That was something I hadn't done since I'd been back in England, and the thought made my stomach grumble. I would have asked Nan if we could have a chippy tea, but when I left hers, her slow cooker was on for a stew, which would, admittedly, be a lot more satisfying.

Following the wall around past the large red rock that stood in the sea, I approached the short row of locked-up beach huts. I headed for the low wall that ran along the edge of the water and leaned my hands down on it, gazing out at the calm waves.

"All of this, it was you who did it. You were the one who pushed for us to be around each other."

The words I'd thrown at her circled around my mind on a never-ending loop. It wasn't untrue, but I hadn't meant to make it sound like I didn't want it; like I didn't want to spend time with her and find some semblance of happiness in a traditional Christmas like the ones I'd once loved.

All the Christmases I'd had as a kid when Nova was no longer in my life were nice, but different. In Italy, we kept doing as many of our usual traditions as we could, but it never felt the same as Christmas in England. Once I left home, I'd forgotten about all of that. I'd grown to love spending the festive season on a beach, and

I'd come to accept that any magic that ever existed was only for kids.

Nova had changed that for me. I'd liked drinking mulled wine with her at the Christmas market. Enjoyed the five minutes of ice skating before I'd slipped on my arse and sprained my ankle. Spending the afternoon with her watching Christmas movies, and how she'd remembered the snacks we used to share. I'd loved baking with her and Nan, and how cute she'd looked when she'd accidentally got a bit of food dye smeared on her cheek. She'd laughed when, instead of wiping it off, I put a matching streak on my own cheek. She made my nan's dark days brighter just with a hug and a smile. She'd shown me there was plenty right there in the UK I didn't know about and had never considered discovering. Against all the odds, she'd made me believe there was still something special about this time of year that went beyond the commercial stuff that had people thinking they needed the perfect turkey or an immaculately dressed tree.

It wasn't Christmas that was magic. It was her.

"Fuck!" I yelled the word out in frustration, smacking my palm down on the wall as I thought about the look on Nova's face when she'd asked me to leave. It was like she didn't recognise me anymore. Deep in her eyes, I saw how much I'd hurt her. I lashed out at her because she'd called me out on the way I'd acted when I first arrived, but she was right. I was selfish, and I hadn't wanted to come. For whatever reason, she'd cared enough to show me things didn't have to be that way. That if I just looked outside of my narrow mind, there was more. Her small town had plenty to offer if I bothered to look. To learn.

Live in the fucking moment. I'd asked her to do that with me knowing full well it was too late for both of us. Something had been building between us, and by the time I kissed her, I was already in deeper than I meant to get. When I looked at her, I thought she could see how much more it was to me than just some passing thing. Instead of letting her know for sure, I'd turned my own issues onto her as if she was the only one who didn't want to let go.

I could tell myself over and over that I lied to her so I didn't ruin her Christmas, but it would have been another lie. My reasons were completely selfish. I truly didn't want her to spend the day thinking about me going away and it dimming her smile and her enjoyment, but mostly, I couldn't face the conversation. I didn't know how to leave her behind, and I still wasn't sure I'd fully accepted the way I was starting to feel about her.

I hadn't been in a serious relationship in seven years. The short relationship I'd had with the girl who was trying to use me hadn't even come close to my time with Paige, and *that* had ended in disaster, with Paige flinging everything I'd ever trusted her with back in my face. I hadn't intended *not* to get into a long-term relationship again, I was just careful, but there were instances over the past few years when I'd wondered if I should have just married Paige because I hadn't felt that spark with any other woman. It wasn't that I compared every woman to her, just that the electricity had been very noticeably missing.

But Nova was different, even from Paige. When she'd appeared on Nan's doorstep, something about her had made my defences shoot up. I'd blamed it on suspicion because, from my experiences, people always want something. But that hadn't stopped me from seeing how attractive she was. Her beautiful eyes, striking cheekbones, and pretty smile. And I felt *something*. It took just one conversation with her to know my concerns about her intentions were unfounded, and every day I spent with her only made me see how special she was.

Now, none of it mattered. In five days, I would leave her behind, and I wouldn't look back.

Couldn't look back.

Christmas was two days away, and... *fuck*.

Christmas.

Nan and I were supposed to be spending the day with Nova and her parents, but now... would that even be possible? We'd made plans to stay over, and her parents were expecting us. Somehow, I didn't think I would be welcome anymore, and even if Nan was pissed off with me—which she would be when she found out what had happened—she wouldn't let me spend Christmas alone. So I might have ruined her day too, at a time that would already be difficult enough.

If nothing else, I needed to make sure Nan had the best day she could, but to do that, I'd have to tell her I'd messed up. Even if I went back to Nova's and apologised, it was too late. I'd destroyed what we had and there was no way to take it back. The best-case scenario was a day of awkward tension, the worst us screaming at each other and Nan and me having to leave early.

The only thing I knew for sure was that I wouldn't let my selfishness ruin anything else. I needed to step up and do what I'd promised my grandad.

I had to be better and do everything I could to make Nan's Christmas the best it could be now it would just be the two of us.

I'D ONLY JUST SHUT NAN'S FRONT DOOR BEHIND ME WHEN SHE CALLED out, "Get in here!"

Shit. Not even the wafting aroma of stew could comfort me when her tone was so sharp.

I walked down the hallway, sensing an impending bollocking, and when I reached the living room, I stood in the doorway, waiting.

Nan was sitting on the sofa, and she peered at me over the top of her glasses. "What's going on?"

She didn't look angry, but the way she'd called me in had made me think she'd spoken to Nova. Her question suggested otherwise. "What do you mean?"

"I saw you leave Nova's house and drive away, and then shortly after, she came out looking upset and drove off too. She isn't back yet, so I guessed you weren't together somewhere, but you two had plans this afternoon. What did you do?"

The fact that it didn't cross her mind that Nova might have been the one who had done something wrong didn't surprise me. Nan adored her, and I might have been her grandson, but she knew full well if something had gone awry, I was most likely to be the problem.

As was my usual way, I clenched my jaw and attempted to remain stoic. "I'm leaving."

Nan's brows furrowed. "Leaving when?"

"On Friday."

"Okay," she said. "And how did that lead to you both storming off in separate cars?"

"Because yesterday I told her I didn't know when I was leaving here, and today, she found out I was lying."

Nan drew in a deep breath and let it out slowly. She didn't speak, just surveyed me as I remained in the doorway, my body tense, waiting for what she was going to say next. The moment seemed to stretch on forever as her disappointment seeped into me.

"I never told her I would stay, Nan," I said, unable to bear the silence any longer.

She shook her head. "That's not what she'll be upset about, and you know it. She thinks the world of you, and even though I know she wants you to stay, she would never ask you to."

Clearly, Nan knew her a lot better than I did. Or maybe not. I always knew she would be angry about the lie, but to ease my conscience, I made it about her not wanting me to go instead of owning up to the fact that I wasn't ready to lose her.

"I know," I said quietly.

"How have you left things?"

"She asked me to leave her house, and I did."

"That was it?"

Shrugging, I said, "I basically accused her of being clingy and said the reason we're in this position is because she pushed to spend time with me. There was no other way to leave it after that."

Saying it out loud, I wasn't sure I'd ever been more ashamed of myself. It was such a dick move to blame her for all of this. To make her think I didn't appreciate every second we spent together. I'd agreed to it. In doing so, I'd fallen for her so hard I was still bouncing.

"Donovan Cain, you need to sort this out immediately," Nan said, standing up and walking towards me.

"I can't." I shook my head. "She won't listen to anything I say now.

Even if I apologise, I can't take back how I made her feel." My chest ached as I said it because I believed it was the truth.

Nan poked me in the chest, right where it hurt, drawing my full attention to her. "You are an idiot, boy. I don't care how you fix it, but you will. Christmas is going to be hard enough without you hurting someone who has shown both of us nothing but kindness and generosity. I can't make you see what is so obvious to anyone else who looks at you both, but you will apologise to her and you will treat her with the same respect she has shown you."

She pushed past me through the kitchen and into the hallway, her footsteps disappearing up the stairs, and I hung my head, letting out a sigh.

I toed my shoes off, kicking them under the kitchen table before heading into the living room to throw myself on the sofa.

My phone vibrated in my jeans pocket, and although I didn't have much interest in speaking to anyone right then, I took it out and looked at the screen.

> **Nova**
> Whether you want to be around me or not, June deserves a good Christmas. Please don't ruin it for her. You both still need to come and spend the day with my family.

She thinks I don't want to be around her? Of course she did. That was exactly the impression I'd given her. Yet, she was willing to put her own comfort aside for my nan, to make sure she had a nice Christmas. Nan deserved more than a half-arsed meal, stuck in her house with only me because of a problem I'd created.

After thinking it over for a moment, I typed:

> Okay. Maybe we shouldn't stay over though. I can drive me and Nan if that makes it easier?

> **Nova**
> That's up to you. Mum says you're still welcome to stay. Depends if you think you can get through the day without drinking.

I smiled in spite of the situation. Good to see her sense of humour was still intact. I guessed from the message that she'd gone to see her mum to let her know what had happened. So, I would be unpopular with just about everyone in the house.

I'd probably need a drink.

I replied:

> Fair point. Better ask your mum to make up the guest rooms then.

> **Nova**
> It's my mother. The guest rooms were made up this morning. :)

Closing my eyes, I let out a groan.

I missed her already. Just like I always did when we'd been away from each other for more than an hour.

And she thought I didn't want to be near her.

I wanted to go sit on her doorstep until she got home and tell her I was a fucking idiot. To take back my dark tone and cruel words. I just didn't believe I had a hope of her trusting me again now.

Instead, I remained where I sat, staring at the messages. After a while, I typed:

> Thank you. :)

The next day without her was going to be a long one, but at least I had a trip to prepare for.

Somehow, that thought didn't make me feel better.

CHAPTER 19

NOVA

As I placed the bag of presents to take to my parents' house in the boot of my car, along with my overnight bag, my stomach churned. I'd barely manage a slice of toast that morning before I got ready because the idea of seeing Donovan was making me uneasy. I knew once I got to my parents' place I'd feel better, but the idea of an uncomfortable drive with him in my car wasn't sitting well with me. I'd made arrangements with June for us to leave at half past nine, and since the moment I woke up, I'd been dreading it.

I hadn't seen or spoken to Donovan since our brief text messages two days ago, and I'd spent Christmas Eve feeling unusually sombre. Every other year, I would have been wrapping up any remaining gifts while watching cheesy Hallmark movies, but the last thing I needed was a bunch of small-town festive romances with a happy ending when I felt so bereft.

The more I thought about the things Donovan had said, the more irritated I'd become. He'd made me feel like I was the only one of us who cared and I'd simply attached myself to him and expected he would magically decide to live out the rest of his life in Devon with me. Life is *not* a Hallmark movie, and I never thought it would be. I *had*, however, expected not to be lied to and made to feel so unimportant.

I shivered as June's front door opened, and she stepped out first, offering me a wave. I tightened my coat around me as she walked towards me. Although she was wearing a coat over her outfit, she looked lovely. She'd had her hair cut the day before, the short style tidied up for Christmas, and she'd even put on a touch of makeup; a little pale pink lipstick and some mascara. I could tell from the tension in her as she hugged me that this day was going to be hard for her, but I held her tight and whispered, "Merry Christmas, June."

"Merry Christmas, my darling. Are you okay?"

Swallowing back an unexpected lump in my throat as I pulled back from her, I nodded. "Yeah. You?"

June sighed. "I think I'm okay. I had a little cry this morning before I got ready, but we'll see how we go."

"We're all here for you," I told her, squeezing her hand.

Just then, my attention was drawn to Donovan, who came out of June's house carrying a bag of gifts and two smaller bags, which I assumed were for their stay. I'd sort of hoped they would change their mind at the last minute about sleeping at my mum and dad's, but obviously, that wasn't to be. He paused on the step to shut and lock the door before pocketing his keys. My breath caught just from the sight of him, my heart rate speeding up with the usual anticipation of being wrapped up in his arms. Then it sank as fast as it had lifted. We were done with that now; my emotions just hadn't caught up with reality yet.

This time, it was June who squeezed *my* hand, and I gave her a grateful smile as Donovan approached. He kept his head down until he reached us, and then he looked up, his eyes meeting mine at last.

The tiniest hint of softness in them made me drop my gaze. I couldn't handle it, not now. Not when he'd made it perfectly clear I didn't matter to him. He hadn't called. Hadn't text. Hadn't apologised.

"All of this, it was you who did it. You were the one who pushed for us to be around each other."

I hoped that wasn't how he viewed today. That this was another way I'd forced him to spend time with me. This particular pre-planned thing was far less about him, and while I'd made that clear when I'd messaged him to ensure they would still come, I wondered if the whole thing was a mistake.

I could feel his eyes on me as I took the bags from him and loaded them into the boot of my car. He didn't glare the way he had the last time I saw him, but if he wanted to talk to me, to make this whole day less awkward, he would have approached me earlier to clear the air. Since he hadn't, I could only assume his position hadn't changed.

"Shall we get going?" I asked, my gaze on June. Considering she was the one who'd lost the love of her life, the empathy radiating from her was warming, but I hated that my hurt must have showed on my face.

"Yes," she said. "Let's go."

AS MUCH AS I'D TRIED TO DROWN OUT THE DISCOMFORT IN THE CAR with Christmas music, there was no hiding it. The air was thick with the tension between Donovan and me, and I couldn't wait to be out of the confined space with him. At least at my mum and dad's house, there were more rooms for me to hide in. None of us had spoken since we got in the car, and as we got out and gathered our things, we only communicated with glances and hand gestures. I began to feel like we were in some kind of silent movie.

June linked her arm through mine in a show of support as we headed for the front door. We hadn't spoken much about what had gone on between Donovan and me, but she had told me in no uncertain terms that she thought he was a pillock; her word, not mine. I didn't want them to fall out because of me, though. It had taken long enough to get them to communicate properly again. However, I did appreciate her understanding.

Mum opened the front door with a wide smile on her face, and she looked amazing. She always made an effort on Christmas Day. She'd twisted her brown hair into an elegant bun, decorated with a little hair clip that had a Christmas pudding on it. She wore a dark green dress that fell to her knees and black tights that had very subtle silver snowflakes woven into them.

"Merry Christmas everyone!" she said as we traipsed inside. She hugged each of us as we entered, even Donovan, which seemed to surprise him.

She did, of course, know all about our argument, but like me, she thought June not feeling lonely was the most important thing. Mum was the kind of person who wouldn't make anyone feel uncomfortable in her home. I kinda loved that about her because I wanted to pummel Donovan with a frozen turkey.

"Come on through," Mum said. "Just drop your bags down in the hallway and we'll sort them out once you've had a drink. Is anyone hungry? I'm just about to make bacon sandwiches."

My stomach grumbled at the idea, and I said, "That sounds good. I can take care of that." I slipped through to the kitchen without another word, letting Mum show June and Donovan into the living room, where I knew my dad would be sitting with a cup of tea. I felt bad for not going to greet him, but I needed two minutes to myself.

My shoulders and neck ached from being so tense, and as I slipped my coat off and hung it on the back of a kitchen chair, I rolled my shoulders, taking a few deep, calming breaths. The kitchen was warmer than the rest of the house due to all the cooking going on, and the aroma of turkey and gammon filled the air, making my stomach growl again.

I had to get my shit together. Had to look at the fling with Donovan as just that. A fun Christmas thing that I could forget about once he left. This day would not be ruined for everyone because of us. Christmas came around once a year, and I wanted to enjoy it.

With the thought solidified in my head, I went to the fridge to find the bacon. Mum had six packs in there, and I assumed some of that was for breakfast in the morning. I opened one pack just as the sound of voices filtered in from the living room. I could hear my dad greeting June and Donovan, and Mum was asking if she could take their coats. She was always such a good host, probably due to the number of business dinners she'd organised for Dad over the years. I made my way to the hob, then located a large frying pan and some cooking oil, laying four strips inside it and firing up the gas.

I stared at the bacon as it gently began to sizzle, breathing in the scent. It was oddly calming, and I jumped when I heard someone say my name.

My mum was standing by the kitchen table, watching me with concern. "Are you okay?"

I nodded, giving her a smile. "I am. I just needed a minute, you know?"

She came over to me and pulled me into a tight hug. "I do, sweetheart. Everyone wants sandwiches and tea, but after that, we can crack open the wine."

Laughing, I said, "Just hand me a bottle and I'll be on my way."

Mum placed her hands on my shoulders as we parted. "Why don't you put the kettle on, and I'll deal with the food. But after that, you're going to need to actually participate in the socialising."

I nodded. "I know. Hopefully, opening presents will help."

"Yeah, we will do that before lunch. I'll put some music on too." She kissed me on the cheek. "Come on, darling. You can get through this."

"Yeah. I can." Rolling my shoulders once more to straighten myself up, I said, "Let's do this."

Within half an hour, we all sat in the living room with our bacon sandwiches and hot drinks, the lights in the windows and on the tree twinkling gently around us as Christmas songs played softly in the background. When I'd first walked into the room, coat and boots removed, Donovan's eyes had fallen on me, and I felt them following me as I handed out the drinks. It was the first time he'd been able to see my outfit. The red jumper dress clung to my curves, and I'd teamed it with a wide black belt with a silver buckle. I wore dangly silver earrings too, which had tiny silver stars on the ends. Like the other women in the room, I'd made an effort with my makeup, and I'd curled my hair the way I had when I'd been out with Gaby and Shannen.

Donovan's eyes on me made my skin tingle, but I pretended I hadn't noticed. As I placed his cup down on the small side table next to the chair he sat in, I glanced at him, instantly wishing I hadn't because, even with such a brief look, his blue eyes glimmered with a warmth I hadn't expected. He was wearing a pair of smart jeans and a black dress shirt; something I'd never seen him wear before, and man, it looked good on him.

Moving away quickly, I tried to get my heart rate under control, but I could still smell him. Coffee and his cool, ocean-like scent surrounded me. My body physically ached with the need to curl up on his lap and breathe him in. Instead, I took a seat on the sofa next to my dad. June was at his other side, and Mum sat on the armchair adjacent to Donovan's, by the window. The Christmas tree was in the corner beside her, and once we were all settled, she slid down to the floor to take charge of the gift giving.

"We'll just do one each for now," she said, and it didn't take a genius to figure out where I got my love of Christmas. She was practically buzzing with excitement, and I smiled at her. She handed me the bag of gifts I'd brought with me, and the one June and Donovan had brought was given to June. "Who wants to go first?"

"Why don't we do some of the ones under the tree?" Dad suggested, sitting forward. Considering we were only a family of three, there was a pretty big pile there. Even factoring in our guests, it was a lot, but this was standard for us. Mum loved giving gifts, and I knew she had bought a few extras for all of us. Everything under the tree was from my parents, and I could see how eager she was for us to see what we'd got.

Mum picked up a rectangular present wrapped in silver foil paper with reindeer all over it, checking the label before handing it to Dad. She then rummaged through until we all had one each, and we began unwrapping them in between sips of tea and bites of our sandwiches.

The one in my hands was big, a little weighty, and rectangular—I'd expected her to start smaller with everyone, but mine was the biggest so far, and I unwrapped it with curiosity, letting out a squeak when I saw what it was.

"Oh my God! *Stranger Things* Monopoly!" I said, giving my first genuine smile since we'd arrived as I hugged it to me. It combined two of my major loves, the hit TV show and Monopoly. I didn't get to play it too often anymore, but board games were a Christmas Day and Boxing Day thing in our family home, and I couldn't wait to get into it. "Thank you so much!"

Mum beamed at me. "You're welcome, sweetheart. Maybe we can play later."

"Nope," Dad said. "No Monopoly on Christmas Day. Anything else is fine, but that takes way too long." He was smiling as he said it, and I knew he was just kidding. He had always loved Monopoly, and we were both super competitive.

I pouted in his direction before laughing and then giving him a hug. "You'll change your mind this afternoon," I teased, and he kissed the top of my head.

"I probably will," he said, then went back to opening his gift, grinning at Mum as a burger recipe book sat in his lap. "Thank you. That's January's tea times sorted out. Burgers every day!"

Laughing, Mum said, "I don't doubt it!"

I could feel Donovan's eyes on me again, but I remained focused on June, who was opening whatever Mum had handed her. It was too small to be the robin ornament, and too big to be the special gift we were saving until later. There was a cube-shaped cardboard box beneath the wrapping paper, and June peeled the tape off and lifted the lid, pulling out some tissue paper, followed by a small snow globe. Inside the globe was a mini scene showing a row of festive-looking buildings, and in front, a couple sitting on a bench with their arms around each other. June's eyes misted over, but she chuckled as she turned it over to make the snow fall.

"This is beautiful," she said. "Thank you." She smiled at my mum then my dad, and he placed his hand over hers.

I knew the reason my mum had chosen that gift, and so did June. She and Trevor had shared the memory with Mum and me last Christmas, both of them roaring with laughter as they spoke.

Donovan, however, wasn't familiar with the story, and he said, "Can I see?"

June handed the snow globe to him. He fixed his eyes on the tiny figures inside, then looked at his grandmother curiously.

June told the story of how she and Trevor got a flight from Italy to London a few years ago after visiting who I now knew to be Donovan's parents. It was snowing, and they got stuck in London. Both exhausted, they'd argued about what they would do. June wanted to stay in the airport and wait for the next flight to Bristol. Trevor said they were lucky to have landed at all and there would be no flights out anytime soon, so they should find somewhere in London to stay for the night. In a stubborn truce, they sat outside the airport on a bench, neither speaking to the other until they were almost frozen solid. At the time, they were both fuming with each other, but they had found it hilarious to look back on.

Even as she told it a second time, June giggled, and Donovan smiled. "It's hard to imagine you and Grandad arguing," he said. "It was mostly just you telling him off."

Nodding, June said, "Yes, I did have to tell him off a lot. He was always being so silly." Her smile faded slightly, and Donovan reached for her hand. My dad was still holding the other, and I looked at my mum.

Without a word, she nodded in understanding and sought out the gift we'd had made for June. It only took a moment, and Mum shuffled across the floor and gave it to her. "We were going to save this for later, but I think now is the right time."

With both hands now free, June began to unwrap the small box, and I also sank to the floor and scooted closer to her. We'd naturally created a cocoon around her because, as much as she would love this gift, it would make her emotional. Even before her fingers had opened the package, a strange wave of grief for Trevor and love for June permeated the room. As she lifted the lid, she raised the box closer to her face. When she caught sight of the photo of her and Trevor engraved on the pendant, she let out a small sob.

"Oh!" She covered her mouth with one hand, the other holding the box shakily. "Oh, this is so beautiful. Thank you."

Her eyes closed as a couple of tears fell down her cheeks, and Donovan leaned over to see what had made his nan cry. She held it towards him, and his eyes glazed over too when he saw what it was. My heart stuttered inside my chest, and a sharp pain tore through me, wishing I could go to him but knowing he didn't want that anymore. I was just an annoyance now. Someone who'd taken whatever we were too seriously, and I breathed deeply, trying to ease the ache taking over my body.

Every one of us had been caught up in a wave of emotion, and I carefully wiped away a tear as Mum knelt up and pulled June into a tight embrace.

"Thank you, Anita," June said. "Thanks, all of you. What a thoughtful gift."

"We wanted you to have a way to keep Trevor close all the time."

June sniffed as they separated. "It's perfect."

"Would you like me to put it on you?" Donovan asked, and June nodded, turning her back to him. He took the necklace from the box and lowered it down in front of her face before doing up the clasp at the back of her neck. Once it was on, June held the pendant between her fingers as if giving her husband a hug.

My eyes drifted to Donovan while he brushed away the evidence of his emotion with his sleeve. Before I lost myself in his beautiful face, I stood, moving to sit back on the couch and sipping my tea.

A warm hand rested on my wrist as I put my drink on the table. June squeezed my arm gently, a gesture of gratitude for the gift, but also with understanding in her eyes. She'd seen the way I'd responded to Donovan's sadness, I knew she had, and she mouthed, "Are you okay?"

My dad looked equally concerned, and I nodded, giving them the most believable smile I could manage. I didn't want any attention on me, and I was grateful when Mum handed Donovan a gift and took one for herself too. I laid my hand over June's, silently thanking her for checking, but then nodded towards Donovan, letting her know he needed her too.

I might have been pissed off with him, but I wasn't heartless.

June winked at me, a gesture of her comprehension, then leaned back, shifting her attention to Donovan, who had just unwrapped a four-pack of Peroni and was eyeing it as if he were considering downing them all in quick succession. After thanking my parents, he placed the drinks down by his feet while Mum opened her present; a pair of gold earrings from my dad.

After a short while, Mum gathered up the plates and cups and sorted out whatever she needed to do in the kitchen. The smell of food coming through was outstanding; I knew we wouldn't have dinner for another few hours yet, though. I wasn't hungry, but the scents were so tempting.

With Mum gone, the balance in the room had shifted. Donovan had taken to looking at his phone, Dad and June were chatting, and I sat in a weird kind of limbo. Donovan caught my attention as he blew out a breath and then began typing something, his fingers moving swiftly across the screen and a frown wrinkling his forehead as he put the phone back on the arm of the chair.

He must have felt me looking at him as he stared at me for a second before reaching forward for the bag of gifts he and June had brought. He rummaged inside before pulling out a wrapped present that was thick and square at the bottom and then narrowed, as if there were two items beneath the paper. He stood, walking over to me, and then sat down cross-legged on the floor by my feet and handed me the gift.

I blinked a couple of times in surprise. "For me?" I asked, glancing at it as if he'd somehow made a mistake.

"Yes. For you." I flicked my gaze between the present in my hand and Donovan once more. "Did you expect me to show up empty-handed?"

"No, but..." I trailed off, unsure how to end the sentence. I'd been so busy focusing on distancing myself from him that I hadn't considered that he might have a present for me. Based on the things he'd said, at most, I thought perhaps I would get something that was from both him and June.

"Open it."

My fingers peeled carefully at the tape that sealed the gold foil wrapping paper, and inside was a jewellery-type box nestled on top of a hinged photo frame that was closed over. I picked up the box and opened the frame. A rush of memories hit me, and I gasped. In one side of the frame was the photo of me, Donovan, and June in our Christmas aprons. But it was the other side that had taken my breath away. A very old-looking photo of me and Donovan as kids, sitting next to the Christmas tree in my childhood home. We were holding hands and grinning, clearly excited for the big day. He did, as he'd said, have slicked-back boyband hair, and my own hair was lighter and hung around my shoulders in curls.

"Where did you get this?" I breathed.

"Mum. After she spoke to us that day at Nan's house, she was convinced she had some photos of us. She video-called her housekeeper and directed her to where all the old photo albums are. She has boxes and boxes of pictures, and she stayed in the call until Juliet had found the ones of us. Then Juliet scanned the photos and sent them to Mum, and Mum emailed them to me."

Words escaped me as I looked at the photos side by side. Past and present. And in both, so happy. Still unable to form words, I placed the still-open frame on the table, glimpsing at it one more time before moving my attention to the jewellery box.

I flipped the lid up and gasped again.

Sparkling up at me were the earrings I'd looked at at Dawlish Christmas Market but had forgotten to go back and buy. I was positive he hadn't bought them on the day, which meant he must have noted the name of the trader then gone to get them for me.

All of this is a lot of trouble to go to for someone he doesn't care about.

I refused to let that thought take hold, still staring at the small snowflakes. "You remembered."

"Yes, I did."

Overwhelmed and a tad confused by his thoughtfulness, I looked down at him again. "Thank you. They're stunning."

He smiled softly. "Nova-"

Closing the lid of the jewellery box, I placed it on the coffee table beside the photo frame and reached into my own bag of gifts, effectively cutting him off. I was too overwhelmed. I also didn't need to hear any guilt-induced apologies, and certainly no kindness from him. This situation was difficult enough without the, 'sorry I hurt your feelings, but this was never really going anywhere' speech. I knew it. Didn't need it reiterating.

Once my fingers had landed on the present I'd been looking for, I forced a smile and passed it to Donovan. Beside me, Dad and June were still talking, but I could sense them occasionally glancing our way. They weren't listening in, but they were keeping a close eye on us.

Donovan turned his present over in his hands once before opening it. It was a brown leather journal, personalised with his initials in gold writing at the bottom left corner, and in the centre, in the same lettering, were the words 'The Travel Hit List'. I'd bought it for him shortly after I'd written the Christmas hit list, wanting him to have something that reminded him of our time together when he moved on. A small part of me regretted getting it since he'd suggested he felt very differently about our time together than I did, but it was personalised for him and I still wanted him to have it.

"I know you write everything online usually, but I thought maybe you could use it to write about things you don't share with the whole world."

He closed the journal again, running his thumb across the leather. Across the words on the front cover. When he finally looked up at me again, he said, "You never expected me to stay."

The words were said as fact, not a question, as if confirming something he had been aware of but hadn't fully comprehended, and his eyes flickered to life the way they used to when he looked at me.

"Nope," I told him. "I didn't. But I think you probably always knew that."

CHAPTER 20

DONOVAN

I SAT THERE, HOLDING THE JOURNAL SHE'D GIVEN ME, MY FINGERS tracing over the cover.

I was such a monumental cock.

She was right. I never thought she'd expect me to stay, and her choice of gift made that clearer than ever. Someone who was trying to keep me here wouldn't have gone to the trouble of getting something so personal made for me; something that related to my job. That wasn't what had surprised me about the gift. The present itself was merely a verification of what I knew, and of what my nan had told me.

What freaked you out about telling her you were leaving, you loser, is that she wouldn't *ask you to stay.*

That thought hit me like a truck. I didn't want to stop travelling. I'd signed a contract for the Maldives job, and I wanted the other potential jobs the company had offered. But I wanted Nova to want me to stay. To want *me.*

I hadn't realised how much my selfish little ego needed her to let me know she felt the same way I did.

Except, she had. The fact my lie had hurt her should have told me all I needed to know.

Over and over since I'd been in Dawlish, I'd witnessed her

selflessness. Giving her time to Nan and me. Keeping her feelings to herself to ensure I didn't think she was trying to trap me in Devon. All of the things she did to make me appreciate a part of my life I'd shunned for so long. There was no need for her to say she felt the same as me because she had shown me every fucking day.

And it still wasn't enough for me. I made her feel like she was in this alone because I was afraid of how much she meant to me.

When I looked up at her, her eyes dropped to her lap, and I hated every bit of pain on her face. Placing my journal on the table, I reached out for her hand, but the second my skin touched hers, she pulled back, her body stiffening.

"Can we please go somewhere and talk?" I asked quietly.

She shook her head, still not looking at me. "I really don't see the point."

Shifting position, I knelt up in front of her so, had she looked up, we'd be at eye level. "Look at me."

Nan and Oliver's conversation had stopped, but it was like they didn't dare move in case they drew attention to themselves. I knew Nova was as aware of them as I was, but I didn't have a problem saying what I needed to in front of an audience if she refused to be alone with me.

"Nova, please." I placed my finger under her chin to gently raise her head.

Tears sparkled in her eyes, and she pushed my hand away and stood up as if she didn't want me to see them. "Don't. I can't..." She stopped, shaking her head again. "I can't."

Getting to my feet too, my large frame blocking her way out, I put my hand on her cheek, brushing away a tear with my thumb, then dropped my arm back down to my side. Her eyes followed the movement so she didn't have to look at my face.

If I'd thought not seeing her for a day was hard, it didn't compare to how excruciating it was to have her so close yet feel so distant from her. And I couldn't even complain about it because I was the one who'd severed the ties. I'd cut her off, not because she had done something wrong but because I couldn't face what I'd fucked up.

Regret had been the theme of the day so far. The theme of my entire visit. Being in England had shed light on all the mistakes I'd made with my family. Showed every way I'd fucked myself over by running away from things I didn't want to deal with because it might be too painful.

It's just as well I travel light because I have enough emotional baggage to last a lifetime.

I'd landed in my hometown, in the house of a woman who'd carried every bit of her grief on her tiny, tired shoulders, and she was still happier than I'd been because she wasn't pretending. She let each day, good or bad, be exactly what it was.

I *was* happy travelling, and I still wasn't ready to stop, but now I could see the things I hadn't admitted. Things I'd learned since I'd been back in England because I'd been forced to open my eyes and look at reality. And that reality hadn't been the picture of the epic traveller I painted myself to be. Some of it was ugly. Repressed grief, lurking memories of angry words spat by my ex, pretending it was okay that I didn't have a place to call home when, really, that was the only thing I'd ever wanted. A base. A safe place.

And then, this bright, beautiful woman sprang up from next door, reminding me of things I'd forced myself to forget. Not just about us as kids, but about myself. About what I loved. What I wanted.

I'd been silent for so long, Nova raised her head to look at me, the tears still sparkling in her eyes, but softer now.

"I need you to listen to me," I said, my voice low, slightly husky from emotion. "Not so long ago, you wrote me a letter, challenging me to re-write Christmas. You wanted me to see our hometown as something more than just a place on the map where I happened to be born. You wanted me to see community, and closeness, and what it's like to have family around. And I did. I saw it all, and I liked it." Risking the smallest shuffle towards her, I said, "Nova, I'm so sorry. For lying to you, and for walking out on you when I had so much more to say. I never meant to make you think I didn't want to do every single thing you planned for us, because there were times I think I wanted it even more than you did." I paused, swallowing down whatever the hell was clogging my throat and taking a deep breath. "I have to leave in four days. I can't change that. And I can't change that I love my job, but I don't want this to end. I don't just mean friending each other on social media and a phone call every couple of months. I want *you*. I have no idea how we would make it work, but that's what I want. And I'm sorry I was too stupid and scared to tell you that sooner."

She opened her mouth to speak, but nothing came out. In her eyes, I could see she still wasn't sure, and my chest throbbed at the realisation my words might be too late. Not enough to make up for placing so much doubt in her mind about how I really felt about her.

"Nova, please," I said again, feeling a tear drip down my cheek. I moved my hand forward a fraction, my little finger hesitantly brushing hers. She looked down, and I watched as one of her own tears escaped and dropped onto the carpet between us.

I was too late.

I started to pull my hand away, but she linked her fingers through mine. Not with any firmness, but enough for hope to rise in me again.

Her eyes met mine, and inside them, I saw a hint of her usual lightness peeking through.

"You made me think you didn't care," she whispered.

Closing my eyes, I breathed, "I know."

"And I didn't... I couldn't understand how I could have been so wrong about the way I thought you felt about me. I thought maybe..." she trailed off, and I tightened my fingers around hers.

"I do," I told her, my gaze holding hers so she knew how much I meant it. "I love you."

CHAPTER 21

NOVA

My breath stuttered. He said it.

Off to the side of me, my dad and June tried to ease themselves out of the room, but there was no way for them to leave subtly. They shuffled out, closing the door behind them, leaving Donovan and me alone.

I moved my gaze back to him, but he wasn't looking at me anymore. His eyes were focused above my head, his jaw clenched and his whole body tense. I could feel his hand shaking in mine as he waited for me to say something.

His beautiful blue eyes were shining, and the hope mixed with defeat that this might already be over nearly brought me to my knees.

I let go of his hand and stepped closer to him, winding my arms around his back, my head against his chest. His heart was racing, and I held him tighter until he crushed me against him, one hand on my lower back, the other buried inside my hair. With a light tug, he prompted me to look up at him, and as I did, his gaze blazed with an intensity I'd never seen before, like everything he'd tried to keep locked away was breaking free.

He'd never been afraid to show affection; that came easily to him.

He hadn't even shied away from letting his guard down around me. But what he had tried to hide from me was how much more I was than a bit of Christmas fun. More than once, I'd believed I meant something to him, but when he'd walked away so easily, those beliefs crumbled away to dust because, if I mattered, he would never have made me feel like I didn't.

But I'd heard him. The things he'd confessed and how he'd found the last couple of days every bit as agonising as I had.

There was no faking the look in his eyes now. No hiding that he was still trembling. Still waiting for me to tell him what he needed to hear. Even though it was happening so fast, everything about it— about *him*—felt right.

"I love you too," I whispered.

Lowering his head, Donovan kissed me as if we'd been apart for years and not days, and as his tongue pressed against my lips, seeking entry, I clung to him. His hands slid down to my hips, drawing them against his.

This was happening. He was with me, and he wanted this. Us.

I was pretty sure if we weren't in my parents' living room, we would have been undressing each other because I couldn't get close enough to him. I wanted to wrap myself around him, feel his hands all over me to make up for the time we'd lost, and for the time that was so quickly slipping away from us. We only had two more full days until Donovan had to leave, and I was nowhere near ready to say goodbye.

I must have pulled away a little because he seemed to sense my mind had drifted off. "*Dolcezza*," he murmured against my cheek. "I'm coming back. I'll always come back for you."

I nodded, any lingering doubts slipping away as his lips found mine again.

What we had, it was so new, and we still had so much to figure out, but I wanted it to work more than I'd ever wanted anything in my life.

"I would never try to make you stay somewhere you don't want to be," I told him. "I hope you know that."

"I know." Donovan brushed his lips across mine. "But we're going to need to be really honest with each other from now on. For the next six months or so, my schedule could be all over the place. I'll come home as often as I can, but if at any point it gets too hard, you need to tell me so I can find a way to make it easier."

Home. He'd called England home. Maybe he meant Dawlish too now he'd become reacquainted with the town.

"As you once pointed out, honesty is not an issue for me," I said, and he smiled, probably remembering his comment from what seemed like a lifetime ago now.

"Very true." Donovan placed a hand on my cheek, resting his forehead against mine. "There are a lot of things we need to talk about, but can it wait until tomorrow? Right now, I just want to enjoy Christmas here with you and our families."

I nodded. "I'd like that too."

WHAT FOLLOWED WAS ONE OF THE BEST CHRISTMASES I'D HAD IN YEARS. Christmas Day with my parents was always fun, but having Donovan and June there too made it perfect. My parents and June were delighted that Donovan and I had sorted things out, and the tension that had lurked earlier disappeared. My mum had made the most incredible Christmas dinner, and we ate until we were stuffed, then went to the living room, where June, Mum, and Dad promptly fell asleep in front of the television, and Donovan and I watched movies until they woke up again. We spent the evening playing board games, all of us laughing the whole time.

June was the first to head to bed at just after nine, and Donovan and I went up closer to ten. When we'd arrived at my parents' house, there wasn't a chance in hell that I'd expected the two of us to share a room, but now, after an amazing day, the only thing I wanted was for us to have some time to ourselves. I went into my room to get ready for bed, while Donovan went to the room he was supposed to be staying in to get his things. In the time he was gone, I went to the bathroom, cleaned my teeth, took off my makeup, and changed into my Christmas pyjamas—a pair of pink trousers covered in Christmas puddings, and a pink vest top with a cartoon-style Christmas pudding on the front.

Donovan had been gone for a while, and as I sat on my bed, I wondered if he'd fallen asleep in his room. I waited for a few more minutes before going to investigate. I knocked softly on his door, and he called out for me to come in.

I opened the door, and my eyes widened at the sight that greeted me. As I took him in, I doubled over, laughing so hard I almost fell over as I walked towards the bed.

Donovan was lying on the bed, feet crossed at the ankles, wearing nothing but a green elf apron, a bit like the ones we'd worn the day we'd baked.

He smiled brightly at me as I staggered over to him, tears of laughter trickling down my face.

"What the hell?" I managed as I climbed onto the bed beside him, and he turned onto his side to look at me.

"We made a deal, remember?"

I cast my mind back to the letters we'd sent each other when Donovan had only just arrived. He'd been so confident he would never enjoy Christmas that he'd promised to dress as an elf if I converted him.

Brows raised, I said, "I won?"

"Yup. And so…" He waved an arm up and down his body, making me laugh again,

"And this was the only elf costume you could find?"

He shook his head. "No, I just thought this would be funnier, and clearly, I was right." Grinning, he wriggled closer to me on the bed.

Holding up a hand, I said, "Wait. We weren't even talking when you packed your bag to come here."

"I know. But I hoped I'd get to show you this anyway. If you hadn't forgiven me, I'd have just thrown it on over my clothes." He paused, tucking my hair behind my ear. "Whatever happened, I wanted to say thank you. When we started the Christmas hit list, I didn't expect to have as much fun as I did. So, even if you'd never forgiven me, I wanted you to know that you made a difference. You made me want a Christmas like this one every year. With you. Sticking to traditions and maybe making some new ones."

Even though my heart was melting at his words, I couldn't help teasing him. "I could get behind you wearing this outfit every year."

Donovan laughed. "Oh, yeah? Do you have a secret elf fetish I should know about?"

Shaking my head, I pressed myself against him and said, "No, I just kinda like that I can get you naked simply by pulling this loop over your head." My fingers reached around to the back of his neck, playing with the strip of material.

He let out a low groan of frustration. "I was trying to be romantic, and you had to lower the tone."

He grinned, letting me know he wasn't really annoyed, but I kissed him gently, and said, "I'm sorry. What you said was sweet, and I would like to spend every Christmas forever creating new traditions with you."

"Forever, huh?"

I nodded. "Yes, please."

Donovan wound his arms around me, then turned onto his back so I was lying on top of him. "I love you," he said, kissing me gently.

I let the sound of those words fill me up. Let them trickle through me and bring back every bit of warmth that had been missing since he'd walked away. "I love you too."

"Lavare i miei calzini sporchi."

As always, the sound of him speaking Italian caused a tingling deep inside me. "I hope that means something romantic."

He smirked. "It means *wash my dirty socks*."

Laughing out loud, I pushed him away playfully. He remembered everything.

Donovan tightened his arms around my back. "Thank you," he murmured, his lips brushing my cheek. "For being the best almost-neighbour I ever had."

He kissed my lips again, and even though we still had a lot to figure out, I didn't want to worry about it right then.

The only thing I wanted to do was be with him, wrapped around him, and living every single second as if we would never get another.

EPILOGUE

NOVA

ONE YEAR LATER

I SAT ON A WIDE, COMFY SOFA, TALL LATTE MUG IN MY HANDS, STARING out at the spectacular view of the Chianti countryside. I'd parked myself in the same spot whenever I got the opportunity over the past week since I'd been in Florence.

As it had been impossible to do so the previous year—and since Donovan hadn't spent Christmas with his parents since he was eighteen—they had invited us to be with them in Italy as soon as the school term ended. Needless to say, I'd jumped at the chance, especially because my parents and June had all been invited too.

Christmas in Tuscany had blown my mind. Louise and Sam had been so kind to us, taking us into central Florence from their renovated country farmhouse, where we'd visited the most epic Christmas market offering gifts and Italian delicacies I'd never tasted before. The city was stunning, as was Donovan's family home. It was set on two floors, and every room was enormous. It had six bedrooms, a main living room, plus two additional rooms off each end, one of which I was sitting in, and the other had been made into a dining room. The grounds of the home seemed to go on forever, and they even had olive trees, and we'd enjoyed the olives many evenings with bread and cheese. *And don't even get me started on the local wine.*

It was New Year's Eve, early afternoon, and Donovan would be back in a few hours. He'd left us the day after Christmas to return to the Philippines, where he'd spent a large part of the end of the year. There had been some kind of problem with his next contract, which would see him spending eight weeks in Thailand from February, and rather than leave it hanging, he wanted to get it sorted out and paperwork signed so it wasn't looming over him. With the awkward travel at this time of year, he had only spent one full day in Manila, where he was meeting with his bosses, before making his way back to Italy.

In the past twelve months, life had been... different. I'd never been in a relationship with someone who wasn't always around, and it had taken a bit of getting used to. Donovan's initial four-week trip in January after we got together led to more work, as I'd expected. Out of twelve months, he'd been in the UK for two of them, and not all at once. He flew back and forth as much as he could, and during the school summer holidays, I'd gone to stay with him in the Philippines for three weeks, which was absolute bliss. It wasn't hard to see why he loved being away; especially at such a luxurious resort. We'd spent some lazy days on the beach, eaten exceptional food, and there may have been several days where we never left our apartment because, although we were in an amazing location, we hadn't spent nearly enough time exploring each other, and that won out every time.

"Hey, sweetheart," June said, as she entered the room with a cup of English tea. It was the only thing she would drink, and she'd brought her own supply with her. Louise followed, and they both sat down on one of the other sofas. I wasn't sure where Sam was, but my parents had hired a car for our stay and gone out to explore the area.

Pulling my attention away from the view, I turned to them, smiling. "Hi. I see you always know where to find me."

Louise laughed. "When we first moved here, I barely moved from that spot for the first year. Even now, the view never gets old."

Louise and Sam had welcomed me with open arms, delighted

186

when they found out Donovan and I were together. When they'd visited Dawlish at Easter, seeing them again had caused a cascade of happy tears, and when my parents had come to see them too, it felt like no time had passed since we'd all been together. Of course, Donovan and I were all grown up now, but our parents connected the way they always had. It felt less like two families joining and more like we had always been one, just separated for a while.

Donovan and I had both gained an extra set of parents, and I'd also gained a grandmother.

June said, "It is a magnificent view." She stared out at the endless green and sighed. "I can't believe we have to go home in a few days. It's gone so fast."

"I know," I agreed. "Back to work for me soon."

Usually, after the Christmas break, I was ready to go back to work, but as much as I missed the kids, I wasn't ready to give up such beautiful surroundings. So much family time had only highlighted how hard the physical distance between us all could be. However, that was something we had had to deal with. Louise and Sam would never move back to the UK, unless such a time came when June needed them to be closer, and that didn't bear thinking about. And my parents were as Devon-obsessed as me, so they weren't going anywhere. I had become slightly more open-minded about living elsewhere, but Dawlish would forever be my first choice.

"You'll soon get back into the swing of things," June said, and she didn't just mean work. Being consistently without Donovan was hard, and while it was our normal, it never really got easier. I always missed him, more rather than less as time passed, but I refused to clip his wings. We'd been in a relationship for just over a year, but we hadn't spent much of it in the same place. In many ways, it still felt new, and my feelings on his job hadn't changed. He was happy, and even though being apart was challenging, as long as he was mine and kept on coming back, I was good with the way things were. Longer-term, we would have to re-assess, and that was something we'd both agreed on, but for the time being, nothing needed to change.

I sighed. "Yeah, I will. Still, I'll miss the epic coffee and pastries here." I raised my mug to emphasise the point.

"Speaking of food and drink," Louise said, "I was wondering if you want to give me a hand in the kitchen. I'm going to start getting some nibbles ready, and Mum tells me you're pretty good at making cookies." She winked at me, making me laugh as I looked at June.

"Your mum's not so bad at it either," I said, remembering the silliness of last year's baking in June's kitchen.

"We can do it together," June said, smiling.

"Is there anything else you want me to make?" I asked. Although it was only a family gathering, we'd decided to make a big deal for New Year's Eve by getting dressed up, having a later-than-normal dinner with four courses, and then music, dancing, and wine until the clock struck midnight.

"You can help with the soup if you want. I'm going to bake some fresh bread too."

My stomach rumbled at the thought. I'd probably put on about seven pounds since I'd arrived, but everything was so delicious. Louise had made bread for Christmas also, and served hot and teamed with butter, it was divine.

"I can do that," I said, smiling.

A COUPLE OF HOURS LATER, LOUISE, JUNE, AND I WERE ELBOW-DEEP IN food prep when I heard the sound I'd been waiting for. The click of the side door into the kitchen, signalling Donovan's arrival. It had to be him as everyone else was already back in the house, and as I turned to him, a red apron covering my clothes and flour all over me, he grinned his wide lopsided smile, and I dropped my cookie cutter and ran to him, leaping into his arms as he kissed me like we were alone. I wound my arms around his neck, breathing him in and finally feeling like the celebrations could begin.

As our lips parted, I laughed, noticing I'd got some flour in his beard, and it was probably also all over his jacket where I was wrapped around him. Giggling, I wiped the dusty white from his face then kissed him again.

"Miss me?" he asked, his eyes shining bright.

"Nope," I teased, wiggling my eyebrows at him because it was fairly clear from the hardness in his jeans that he had missed me, and my pouncing on him hadn't helped.

"Urgh, both of you get out of my kitchen," Louise joked as Donovan's lips found mine again.

I dropped my legs from around him, turning to look at her, knowing my cheeks were flushed. "I can finish helping in here first," I said, my cheeks flaming more at what I'd said.

First meaning, before I go upstairs and have sex with your son.
Subtle, Nova.

June and Louise glanced at each other, contagious smiles on their faces. "Get out of here," June said, shooing us away with her hand. "We'll see you at dinner time." She shook her head, chuckling.

"Thanks, Nan," Donovan said, looking both amused and embarrassed that his grandmother had given us permission to get naked for the next five hours. He grabbed my hand and dragged me out of the kitchen and up to our room.

JUST AS JUNE HAD PREDICTED, WE DIDN'T EMERGE UNTIL FOOD WAS ready. We weren't doing it the *whole* time. There was some conversation, and then a shower, and then getting ready, but needless to say, it had been a fun afternoon.

Dinner with our family was truly exceptional. We'd all chipped in in some way to make the dinner, but Louise had done most of the work, and it was outstanding. The drinks and conversation flowed easily, and once we had eaten and everything had been cleared away, Sam turned the music up and we all spread out to do our own thing for a while. Mum and Dad were drinking wine together in the living room, Sam was dancing with June in the room we'd all sat in earlier, and Louise was making sure enough nibbles were scattered around for everyone.

Donovan and I stood outside on the small balcony on the second floor, looking out at the dark night, the garden lights offering a subtle glow from below.

I shivered slightly as a cool winter breeze drifted around us, and Donovan took off his black dinner jacket to wrap around my shoulders. He always looked good to me, but he could rock formal attire like nobody else, and I smiled up at him as his scent cocooned me.

He pulled me close to him, his hands gliding across the midnight blue fabric of my long dress.

"I have to tell you something," he said, pressing a kiss to the top of my head and holding me tighter.

Something in his tone made me nervous, and although I could feel my muscles growing tense, I didn't move away, I just waited.

"There was no problem with my contract for my next job," he admitted, grimacing slightly, and my brow furrowed.

"Then... where did you go?" I asked, my heart rate slowly gaining speed. *And why is he only telling me now?* It must have been pretty important if he'd left his family behind.

"I did go to Manila. But it wasn't because of a problem. It was..." he paused, taking a deep breath. "I went to terminate the contract."

I leaned back slightly, tilting my head to the side. "What? Why?"

"Because I got a better offer."

My heart dropped into my stomach, setting off at a gallop. Was he about to tell me we would be spending even more time apart next year? I never interfered in his job, but for this whole year, we'd always talked over where he was going before he signed anything. This sounded different somehow.

"What offer?" I asked, trying to keep my voice steady.

"It's this idea I've been thinking about for the last few months." His lips pulled up very slightly at the corners, so little I wouldn't have noticed if I hadn't been watching his mouth so intently, awaiting his next words. "Sometime last year, I ended up in this little town. Got to know one of the locals. She showed me some cool places in the area and suggested I could maybe see some more of them if I wanted to travel somewhere different for a change." He grinned as my eyes widened, and he continued, with fake self-importance, "I told her I was *far* too special to slum it in England, and-"

I whacked his shoulder as he started to laugh, moving his hands around to my waist and dragging me close to him again. "Donovan! What are you saying?"

"I'm coming home. Kind of. I've decided that, in the coming year, I'm going to trawl the corners of the UK and let people know the best, quirkiest parts. So, I'll still be on the road, but I will be home every weekend, and I thought we could even do some stuff together at the weekends and when you're on school holidays."

"But..." I began. "You wanted the other contract. I thought the money..."

He shook his head, interrupting me. "The money isn't important. I won't make as much in the UK as I did this year, but I didn't need it anyway. It was a bonus, but not the reason. I just wanted the experience. Now, I need to be where you are. If you'll have me."

I blinked, shock short-circuiting my brain because of all the things he could have said, that ranked lower than him running off to join the circus.

"Will you?" he asked, doubt glimmering in his eyes at my lack of response. I could practically see him doubting not discussing it with me beforehand, and I shook my head, reaching up to place a hand on his cheek.

"Yes," I told him. "Of course I will, but... just know it'll be harder for me to let you go after a year together." I smiled because even though it was the truth, if he wanted to go out into the world again, I wouldn't stop him.

"I'm not planning to be away for any length of time again, *dolcezza*," he said as I slid my hand to the back of his neck. "Anywhere else I go, I want to go with you."

There was no way to stop the smile from breaking out on my face, but I had to just check one thing before I got too excited. "Are you sure about this? I want you to do this for you, not because you think it's what I want."

He shook his head, his eyes intense on mine. "I'm done with long distance and longer trips. This was my eleventh year of travelling, and I want to be closer to you now."

"Okay, but if you change your mind-"

He silenced me with a kiss. "Nova. I've been on the road for a long time. There were places I loved and had the best times, but I was still always thinking about where I would go next. I love my mum and dad, but every time I visited them, I had my mind on getting away somewhere else within a couple of days. When I'm with you, there is nowhere else I want to be. The places I've been to since I've been with you were some of the best ever, but I wanted to come home. It physically hurts to be away from you for too long." He smiled, looking deeper into my eyes to offer reassurance. "I won't change my mind. My future is with you."

Gazing up at him, my eyes wet with happy tears, I said, "Seems like you've put a lot of thought into this."

"I didn't need to." He placed a kiss on the end of my nose, then another on my lips. "I've wanted this since the first time I told you I love you, and that isn't going to change until I take my last breath."

My heart swelled, entirely full in that moment. I hoped our last breaths were a substantially long time away because I felt the same. Like the moment those words first left our lips, we'd already begun to re-write our futures so they aligned instead of ripping us away from each other. Now, nobody could do that.

Now, we'd both found our home.

Not next door, but together at last.

The End

AUTHOR'S NOTES

Thank you so much for reading Re-Writing Christmas! I hope you love Nova and Donovan as much as I do!

What you may or may not know is that Dawlish is my hometown. I grew up there and lived there for most of my life. It's a beautiful town on the South Coast of England, and I wanted to write this little love letter to one of the best places in the whole world. I may live elsewhere now, but South Devon is a place where I hold so many memories. Of places and of people and of amazing times as both a child and an adult. If you've never been there, I highly recommend a visit to see the points of interest I mentioned within the story. You truly haven't lived until you've sampled Gay's Creamery ice creams!

Although my next book is mostly unrelated to this story, you will see Nova and Donovan again in it. I'm sure you'll remember Nova's friends, Shannen and Gaby, who work at the same school as her. Next up will be Shannen's story, and you can find out more about that here: https://books2read.com/allyou

Finally, if you would be so kind as to leave a review for Nova and Donovan, please do so on your favourite ebook retailer platform. Reviews mean the absolute world to indie authors, and we appreciate every single one!

If you would like to keep in touch you can do so by following me on Facebook, Instagram, or TikTok, or signing up for my mailing list.

You are also welcome to join my Ream Community, where you can get early access to the novels I'm writing, plus a whole bunch of other perks!

ABOUT THE AUTHOR

Kyra Lennon is a British romance author who has published several books in the contemporary romance genre. She began her writing career in 2012 with her debut novel Game On and has since published several other books, including the Chaos and Consent duet.

Lennon's writing is known for its relatable characters, emotional depth, and compelling storylines. Her books often explore themes of love, loss, and self-discovery, and are generally well-received by readers for their heartwarming and engaging nature.

In addition to her writing, Lennon is also an avid reader and blogger, and has been involved in the online book community for several years. She is active on social media and maintains an active presence on platforms like Twitter and Facebook, where she interacts with her readers and fellow authors.

OTHER BOOKS BY KYRA LENNON

Chaos and Consent Series

Hear What You Want

Say What You Feel

Standalones

Reasonable Doubts

Unintended

Picture (Im)Perfect

Printed in Great Britain
by Amazon

45956311R00112